Reckless

Reckless

Keisha Ervin

www.urbanbooks.net

Urban Books, LLC
97 N18th Street
Wyandanch, NY 11798

ISBN 13: 978-1-60162-609-7
ISBN 10: 1-60162-609-6

First Mass Market Printing August 2014
First Paperback Printing September 2012
Printed in the United States of America

10 9 8 7 6 5 4 3 2

This is a work of fiction. Any references or similarities to actual events, real people, living or dead, or to real locales are intended to give the novel a sense of reality. Any similarity in other names, characters, places, and incidents is entirely coincidental.

Distributed by Kensington Publishing Corp.
Submit Wholesale Orders to:
Kensington Publishing Corp.
C/O Penguin Group (USA) Inc.
Attention: Order Processing
405 Murray Hill Parkway
East Rutherford, NJ 07073-2316
Phone: 1-800-526-0275
Fax: 1-800-227-9604

Reckless

by

Keisha Ervin

A woman has got to love a bad man once or twice in her life to be thankful for a good one.

—Mae West

Chapter One

The only one who made me cry is you.
—Keri Hilson, "Toy Solider"

"Girl, is that him?" Farrah's roommate and business partner, London, tapped her shoulder.

Farrah gazed across the room and spotted her ex-boyfriend, Khalil. Frozen stiff, she struggled to breathe. Every limb in her body seemed to be placed on lock. She knew this moment would come eventually. She just never expected it to happen that night.

She wasn't prepared to deal with the never-ending drama between her and Khalil but, fuck it. Her mama didn't raise no punk. There was no way she could pass up a golden opportunity to confront him.

During their four-year relationship she'd been Khalil's lover, friend, confidant, mother, provider, and more. With him, Farrah had gone through every aspect of hell there was. He'd lied, cheated, and disregarded her feelings but Farrah loved him despite it all.

She loved him despite the fact that he'd cheated on her with his ex-girlfriend, Keisha, the same Keisha who was his high school sweetheart. She loved him despite the fact that one of his ex's called their house on more than one occasion to speak to him. She loved him despite all of the times she caught him text messaging other chicks in the middle of the night.

Farrah loved him despite all of the times he lied to her about being with his pot'nahs when really he was with other females. She loved Khalil despite all of his mood swings, him destroying things in a fit of rage, his excessive spending habits, and irresponsible behavior. She loved Khalil with parts of her body she didn't even know existed. All she knew and could see was him, despite her family and friends' disapproval of their relationship. She truly believed that with time, patience, and love he'd change, but all the love in the world couldn't save Khalil from himself. He was a self-destructive, irresponsible, selfish weed head, alcoholic, BMX rider who hadn't won a tournament in years. The more he lost the more he resented Farrah, whose career as a celebrity stylist was on the rise.

Without blinking, Khalil's insecurities and fuck-ups became Farrah's problems and his problems became his excuse to treat her like shit. But Farrah was done tolerating nonsense and heartache just to have someone there to hold her at night. She was tired of carrying his trifling ass. Sure, a woman was supposed to hold her man down but damn was she supposed to pay the rent and bills, and be his maid, psychologist, personal chef, freak in the sheets, and mother to his immature ass all at the same time? Hell no!

Whenever Khalil fucked up by blowing his money on cars, clothes, and jewels she was right there to pick up the pieces, which would then set her back financially. Khalil didn't care though. As long as he was good that was all that mattered. It didn't matter that Farrah constantly had to worry about how the rent and bills were going to get paid.

Khalil was about living life in the fast lane. He didn't worry about what tomorrow had to bring because he knew that Farrah would never let him fall. After a while his careless behavior began to catch up with him. All of the late nights out partying and heavy drinking started to affect his career. Within a blink of an eye his career was over, and he was left with nothing but a drinking problem and a bruised ego.

Farrah tried to lift his spirits with words of encouragement but Khalil was immune to her kindness. All he saw was that he'd hit rock bottom and that Farrah was on top. Over time the resentment that permeated his soul began to seep out the more he drank, and one drunken night he told her all of her hard work and good fortune wouldn't last long and that she wasn't shit.

Little did Khalil know, that would be their last and final showdown. Farrah didn't have to take his crap so she did something she should've done years before. She chucked his ass up the deuce and told him to step. But being the bitch-ass nigga he was, instead of dealing with the breakup like a man, Khalil lost his damn mind and tore up all of her things in a rage. Couch, bed, television, you name it he destroyed it. After attempting to get him to pay for the damages to no avail, a month passed and Khalil refused to give her back her house keys or come get the rest of his shit.

Even though he was physically gone it was like he still had control over her life and Farrah was sick of it. It was time for her and Khalil to end things once and for all. Dressed in a blue jean jacket, vintage AC/DC T-shirt, black leggings, and five-inch stilettos, Farrah strutted across the room. Normally, she wouldn't have been caught dead in such a getup but that night she'd planned on being laid-back. Thankfully, her mesmerizing good looks made up for her less-than-stellar outfit.

Farrah was a five-foot-three, 105-pounds, bronze-colored beauty with a face that resembled an angel. Her radiant bronze-colored skin complemented her slanted eyes, button nose, rosy cheeks, and pink pouty lips. Being the edgy fashionista she was, she rocked the right side of her hair shaved low like Cassie, while the rest of her long, silky black hair cascaded down her back.

Pure adrenaline rushed through Farrah's veins as she inched closer to Khalil. Kanye West's mega hit, "All of the Lights," blasted through the speakers, hyping up the crowd around her. "Turn up the lights in here, baby. All of the lights so y'all can see this." Rihanna sang the hook. The closer she got, the more Farrah felt as if she were having an out-of-body experience.

After not seeing Khalil for a month, she naturally assumed she'd still feel some sort of attraction, or compassion, for him but all she felt was resentment and hate. His ass couldn't bother to buy a roll of toilet tissue or buy her a Happy Meal when they were together, but had the nerve to be posted up in the club like he was hot shit.

Pissed, Farrah pushed her way through the crowd before his pot'nah P, whom she'd spotted, had the chance to warn him. Face-to-face she looked Khalil square in the eyes and said, "Give me my keys."

Khalil gazed back at her with a glossed-over look in his eyes. It was obvious that he was high and stunned to see her.

"Give . . . me . . . my . . . keys," Farrah stressed, trying to steady the heartbeat in her clit.

Khalil was a complete asshole but he was fine as hell. His even, cocoa-colored skin complemented well his locks that reached his shoulders. Deep brown eyes, goatee, and full lips that were now the color of his skin from smoking too much weed made up his facial features. He was only five-foot-nine, but his arrogant attitude and impeccable taste for fashion made up for his lack of height.

Every time she looked at him she often thought of the rapper Wale. The two could have easily been long-lost brothers. Farrah couldn't front; Khalil was murdering every other nigga in the club that night. On his head he rocked a Louis Vuitton baseball cap cocked to the right. The rest of his outfit consisted of a red and black checkerboard-print button-up, dark jeans, and a pair of Space Jam Jordans.

"I don't have 'em," he finally responded.

"Really, Khalil?" Farrah cocked her head to the side.

She was so sick of him playing childish, immature games. Khalil kept all of his keys on a key chain located directly on his hip.

"I don't have 'em on me," he lied, placing his drink down on the table beside him. "And you don't have to worry. I'm not gon' walk up in yo' house," he said sarcastically.

"Oh, I know you won't. You don't have the balls to," Farrah shot back. "So when are you going to come get the rest of your stuff?"

"I don't give a fuck about that shit." Khalil waved her off. "You can throw it away for all I care."

"You are a fuckin' trip," Farrah scoffed with a look of disgust in her eyes.

"Ay yo, you a'ight?" P came over and asked as if he were Khalil's bodyguard.

Farrah eyed P in shock. This was the same nigga she allowed to sleep on her couch, invited over for dinner, and now he had the nerve to play her out like she wasn't shit.

"Look, can I talk to you in private?" she snapped with an attitude.

"What?" Khalil screwed up his face.

"I said"—Farrah pulled him by the back of his neck so he could hear her better—"let me holla at you!"

As if she were some sort of groupie, Khalil pulled away from her grasp and shot P a look as if to say, "Get this thirsty bitch away from me." The gesture alone made Farrah feel two feet tall. She couldn't believe he had the audacity to disrespect her like that after everything she'd said and done. During their relationship, Farrah had confessed her undying devotion to him and been his ride-or-die chick. She'd stood by his side when his family and friends hadn't supported him, tolerated his crap, shed galloons of tears for him, nurtured him, consoled him, and encouraged him.

She'd been every woman for him. She'd given her all to him and to have him sit there with an evil, smug expression on his face was all Farrah could take. Before she knew it she'd picked up his drink and tossed it over his head. Farrah didn't even bother staying around to see his reaction. She'd gotten her issue off so nothing else had to be said or done. Heading out the door, she held her head up high like the diva she was. Little did she know, Khalil was hot on her trail.

"What the fuck you throw a drink on me for?" he barked angrily.

"'Cause you fuckin' deserved it!" Farrah spun around and looked at him. The drink she'd poured on him trickled down his face like rain.

"That shit wasn't necessary!" Khalil pushed her into the middle of the street. "I swear you's a silly bitch! That's why I don't fuck wit' yo' ass now!" He pushed her again, almost causing her to lose her balance.

"Are you fuckin' deranged? I left yo' tired-ass alone!" Farrah pushed him back as hard as she could.

"Fuck you!" Khalil tried spitting in her face but ended up only making a farting nose with his mouth.

"You are such a bitch!" Farrah hawked up as much spit as she could and showed him how it was done. A wad of spit landed directly in the center of Khalil's face.

"Ay, Khalil! Chill out, man!" P said, trying to pull him back.

"Nah, fuck her! She gon' throw a fuckin' drink in my face!" Khalil yelled as Farrah turned to walk to her car.

But she didn't even make it five feet before she went flying to the ground. Khalil had pushed her in the back. Lying on her side she looked up at Khalil, who was standing over her. She just knew that he was going to kick her but he didn't.

Instead he continued to berate her like she was a child.

"Stupid bitch! I'll fuckin' kill you!" Khalil shouted as P and the doorman pulled him back.

Livid that he would push her when her back was turned, Farrah got up off the ground and kicked off her heels. She was over being Khalil's punching bag. She'd taken enough shit off of him to last her a lifetime. Now was the time to show him what she was really made of. Charging toward him, Farrah remembered all the times he'd cussed her out, made her cry, the females calling her house, the condoms she'd found in his pocket, the hole he'd punched in her wall, and the time he'd called her cunt.

Filled with rage, she balled up her fist and punched him in the face with so much power his head jerked back. Even P and the doorman who were trying to restrain Khalil were surprised at the force of the punch.

"Push me again, muthafucka!" Farrah spat, amped.

"You fuckin' crazy, bitch? I'll murder yo' ass!" Khalil broke loose and charged toward her.

Farrah never thought she'd be that chick fighting outside the club, but she'd come too far to back down now. Khalil was going to learn that he'd fucked over the wrong chick. Before he could get his hands on her, Farrah punched him again, directly in the jaw. Once again caught off guard by her strength, Khalil grabbed her by her jacket only to get socked in the mouth. A trail of blood slid from the corner of his lip.

"What the fuck is wrong wit' you?" He shook her, bewildered.

"You're my problem!" Farrah punched him again. "Wit' yo' punk ass!"

"Khalil, man, let her go," P yelled. "The police coming!"

Shaken, Khalil released Farrah from his grasp. He and the police didn't mix. Khalil had warrants out for his arrest all over St. Louis.

"I swear to God I shouldn't have never fucked wit' yo' crazy ass!" He ice grilled her.

"My sentiments exactly!" Farrah smiled. "Bye, bitch!" She waved as he walked away.

"Oh my God, girl! What happened?" London raced outside. "One of the dudes inside said you was out here fightin'! Did that muthafucka hit you?" London examined Farrah's face.

"Girl, I'm all right," Farrah said, wiping dust off of her.

"Uh-ah." London shook her head. "Where that punk-ass nigga at?" She snatched off one of her heels.

"Girl, put yo' damn shoe back on." Farrah laughed.

"You sure? 'Cause I'll fuck his ass up," London said, ready to pounce.

"I'm sure. C'mon, girl. Let's make like a big titty and bounce." Farrah linked arms with London.

After picking up her heels, Farrah and London walked to her car and hopped in. Farrah hadn't felt this alive in years. It felt good to finally stick up for herself. From then on, she vowed to never allow a man to treat her like dirt. She deserved better. She was a good-ass woman and some man out there would eventually appreciate her for the queen she was. Until then, she was content with doing her and moving forward with her life.

Starting the engine, she pressed play on the CD player. Nicki Minaj's "Shitted On 'Em" started playing. A huge smile spread across her face. Immediately, she turned up the volume and pulled away from the curb while she and London sang, "Man I just shitted on 'em! Put yo' two fingers in the air if you did it on 'em!"

Chapter Two

I should go but I can't overcome this chemistry.
—Britney Spears,
"He About To Lose Me"

Since her and Khalil's breakup, Farrah felt like she'd been run over by a Mack Truck. Yeah, she'd gone all *Bad Girls Club* on his ass, but the fact still remained that underneath all the anger, hurt, disappointment, and hate she still missed him, and it hurt like hell that he didn't miss her too. After four years of being together, he hadn't even called once to say he was sorry or to see if she was okay.

Yet, from time to time Farrah wondered what he was doing and if he ever did think of her. *I am fuckin' pathetic,* she thought, gazing at a picture of him. Hating that thoughts of Khalil still entered her mind, she headed toward the kitchen. She figured drinking her misery away would help erase thoughts of him from her memory bank.

But before she could open the fridge the doorbell rang.

"Who is it?" she yelled, walking toward the door.

"Me," London said dryly.

"Where the hell is yo' key at?" Farrah asked sarcastically, unlocking the door.

"I left it on the table." London dragged her feet up the steps.

"What's wrong wit' you?" Farrah followed her.

"My damn feet hurt. I just did seven bridesmaids' faces, the bride's and groom's mothers' faces, two cousins, and the bride's face. I am tired. Do we have any wine left?" London plopped her purse down on the kitchen counter.

"You know we do."

"Well, pour me a glass immediately. 'Cause in about 10.2 seconds I'ma be on the floor cryin'." London poked out her bottom lip.

"Girl, I was just about to open up a bottle 'cause I was feelin' the exact same way." Farrah pulled out a bottle of Chardonnay and poured them both a glass.

"You wanna go sit out on the patio?" she asked.

"Yeah." London picked up her glass and followed Farrah outside.

The sun was just beginning to set. A pink hue covered the sky and not a cloud was in sight. The setting was perfect. Farrah sat down in a comfy wicker chair and crossed her legs. Relishing the warm weather, she took a much-needed sip of wine.

"Mmm . . . I needed that." She tilted her head back and gazed up at the sky.

"What's yo' issue?" London tapped her on the leg. "Spill the beans, bitch."

"I really don't wanna tell you. 'Cause I already got a piss-poor attitude and I don't feel like hearing yo' mouth." Farrah sighed, rolling her eyes.

"What?" London's eyes bucked. "I swear to God no judgment."

Farrah took a deep breath and wondered if she should open up to London. It was a well-known fact that she didn't like Khalil, so Farrah knew that she wouldn't be sympathetic to the way she was feeling.

"All right, look." Farrah finally caved in. "I feel stupid for even sayin' this out loud but I'm kind of starting to miss Khalil a li'l bit."

"And you should feel stupid," London interjected.

"Heffa, you said no judgment," Farrah snapped.

"Okay." London held up her hands as if to say she surrendered.

"Look, I know that how he's treated me hasn't been right—"

"You ain't got to tell me twice," London cut her off.

"But, for four years he's all I've known."

"And, Tina was wit' Ike for damn twenty but she got over it. Look . . ." London situated herself in her seat. "We've already had this conversation too many times to count. You know I don't like Khalil. He plays way too many games for me. And I mean let's keep it one hundred." London eyed her friend. "How many times has he cheated on you? I don't understand why you keep tryin' with this dude. Hell, I'm living here now 'cause he won't help you with the rent and his name on the lease," London stressed.

"'Cause I love him and technically he only cheated on me once—"

"Twice, to be exact," London chimed in. "You remember Alisha don't you?"

"Okay, bitch, he cheated on me twice," Farrah shot. "But, what you don't understand is that we have a connection. I mean, yeah, at times he can be an asshole but what we share is deeper than what people think."

"That sound good on paper but actions speak louder than words. The man not only played the shit out you but just tried kickin' yo' ass outside of a nightclub a week ago," London stressed. "So, y'all connection ain't that deep if you ask me."

"Well, I didn't." Farrah rolled her eyes. "And, if I remember correctly, couldn't nobody tell you shit when you was wit' Amir."

"But, the thing is I learned from my shit," London shot back.

"Heffa, please." Farrah waved her off. "If Amir called you right now you'd be back wit' him in a heartbeat. Who you think you foolin?"

"Yeah, okay. Honey, I don't get sprung, I spring." London rolled her neck.

"Mmm hmm." Farrah sucked her teeth.

"Whatever. You want some more wine?" London stood up.

"Nah, I'm good," Farrah said, feeling salty.

She despised the fact that London knew her so well. Secretly, she feared that if Khalil tried, or begged hard enough, she'd break and take him back. The fact that London picked up on her weakness ticked her off. She wanted to be strong and act like she was good with being alone, but Farrah couldn't shake missing and wanting Khalil.

"Check it," London said, sashaying back outside. "I know that things have been rough so why don't we kiss all of our troubles good-bye and have a girls' night out on the town?"

"That's cool," Farrah replied, trying to put her feelings aside but finding it hard to. "As long as we don't go to Lola. I don't think I'll be allowed in the building for a while." She laughed.

"We'll go to EXO then," London said.

"Question?" Farrah ignored her friend's suggestion. "Is it really that weird that after all the shit he's put me through I still have feelings for Khalil?" Farrah stared off into space.

"No." London shook her head profusely. "You all did have a four-year relationship and you loved him. That shit don't just go away in a matter of weeks. Hell, it might never go away. You may always feel something for him. But that doesn't mean that you have to act upon those feelings, or be wit' him. Listen." London turned to her friend and leaned forward. "Don't let the shit I said get to you. You know me. I'm an asshole. I think this time you're done with Khalil for good. But you just have to believe it."

London was right; Farrah couldn't continue to let the pain she felt inside get the best of her. What she'd experienced was horrible but she couldn't allow herself to stay in that negative space forever. Khalil was going to forever be Khalil. There was no changing him. The only person Farrah could change was herself and she couldn't continue to dwell on the past. Their relationship was over for a reason. A new beginning for Farrah was approaching. She just had to be open to receiving it.

"Got one question, one question for you. When I'm going through withdrawals tell me what I'm supposed to do?" Farrah sang, throwing her hands up in the air while moving her torso like a snake.

Diddy-Dirty Money's hit song "Your Love" was her shit. It was the perfect song to get her out of her funk. Feeling herself in a gray sweatshirt, red satin mini skirt, and black closed-toe Brian Atwood ankle boots, Farrah popped her booty. Her hair was styled cutely in an abundance of wavy curls. She was looking good and feeling even better. The men around her must've thought so too 'cause they were all over her.

Farrah loved all of the attention she was getting. It felt good to know she still had it. London, on the other hand, never forgot the hold her beauty had on men. Shorty was a ten and the white tank top with a black pistol on the front, white tutu, and black combat boots she rocked proved it. Dancing back-to-back the two friends let all of their inhibitions and stress from the week out onto the dance floor when, suddenly, some random guy dressed in a muscle shirt and slacks rolled up on Farrah and started dancing.

"Oh my God." She spun around and faced London.

"Do you know the Incredible Hulk?" London asked.

"Hell no." Farrah continued to dance as another guy with a gold tooth slid between them and started doing the Stanky Legg.

"Uh oh! You see me doing it? You see me?" he yelled, moving his leg back and forth.

"Oh my God. I'ma throw up." London pretended to gag.

Completely outdone, Farrah stood stunned as the two guys joined hands and started dancing around her and London in a circle.

"Don't you go nowhere!" the guy in the muscle shirt said. "Circle of love, girl! Circle of love!"

"This is not happening." Farrah placed her head down and laughed.

"Oh, but it is." London grabbed her friend's hand and whisked them both away.

"Oh, so that's how it is? You just gon' break the circle of love?" the Stanky Legg guy shouted over the loud music.

"Pretty much!" London shouted back. "WTF. They were such circus freaks."

"Right," Farrah agreed. "If this is what I got to look forward to then I might as well be back with Khalil's ass. At least I know his drama."

"Over my dead body." London scrunched up her forehead. "Come to the bathroom with me." She pulled her friend.

"No. I want a drink." Farrah stopped mid-stride.

"Ooh me too. Get me a Patrón margarita."

"A'ight, meet me at the bar." Farrah grooved her way through the crowd when someone reached out and grabbed her hand.

Please, God, don't let this be muscle shirt guy 'cause I don't feel like cussing his ass out, she thought before looking to see who it was trying to get her attention. Farrah gazed to the right and found Corey Mills, aka Mills. Mills was one of Khalil's close friends. Over the years Farrah had always found him attractive.

He was every girl's wet dream. He was tall, around six-foot-two. His butter-colored skin reminded her of the sun. Farrah instantly fell in love with his boyish good looks. His low haircut, thick eyebrows, sparkling brown eyes, full lips, and goatee were a complete turn-on.

The numerous tattoos that blessed his neck, chest, back, and arms only added to his sex appeal. And when he flashed his mega-watt smile she melted every time. He and Chris Brown could've been identical twins but Mills's swagger was off the Richter scale. That night he looked good as hell in a black White Sox baseball cap, black wafer shades, platinum rosary, fitted white tee, black jeans, and black Chuck Taylors. Unlike Khalil, Mills was one of the country's top BMX riders. He had endorsements from Gatorade and Nike.

People in the sports world and entertainment respected him. He'd turned his lucrative career as a BMX rider into a gold mine. Mills had begun a custom bike collection, clothing company, and tattoo shop. Women adored him and men feared him and Mills wouldn't have it any other way.

"What you doing here?" He took off his shades and looked down at her seductively.

Farrah could tell by the look in his eyes that he was high.

"Same thing you are." She smiled back.

"I heard about what happened between you and my homeboy." Mills pulled her close. "You good?" He stroked her cheek.

"Yeah, I'm a'ight." Farrah looked off to the side nervously.

"You know you too pretty to be carrying on like that. What I tell you? Don't let no nigga take you off yo' square."

"Oh, I'm pretty huh?" Farrah locked eyes with his and grinned.

"Too pretty if you ask me." Mills licked his bottom lip.

Is this nigga flirtin' wit' me? Farrah wondered. *Nah, he couldn't be. He's Khalil's friend. He wouldn't do no shit like that.*

"Who you here wit'?" Mills asked, interrupting her thoughts.

"Umm." Farrah blinked. "My friend, London."

"That's what's up. I thought you might be here wit' yo' new man or something." Mills grinned, still holding her hand.

"Ay." London tapped Farrah on the shoulder. "I'm gettin' ready to go. Amir just called."

Farrah simply shook her head and chuckled. London was making a huge mistake by messing back with Amir, but London would have to learn that lesson the hard way.

"What?" London arched her eyebrow.

"Do you, boo." Farrah waved her off. "Uh, London, you remember Mills don't you?"

"Yeah. How you doing?" London reached out her hand for a shake.

"I'm good, you?" he asked, shaking her hand.

"I'ma be real good when I met up with this li'l daddy," London joked, doing the Dougie. "Speaking of li'l daddies," she whispered in Farrah's ear. "You better get on this one. He is a tender."

"No, he's Khalil's friend," Farrah whispered out of the side of her mouth.

"Please, fuck Khalil. You don't owe that nigga nothin'. You better do you, 'cause he for damn sure doing him," London stated.

"Weren't you leaving?" Farrah responded in her normal voice.

"As a matter of fact I am," London replied, as Amir called her phone.

"I'm on my way out now," she said, not bothering to say hello.

"On that note, deuces." London threw up the peace sign and sashayed down the steps and out the entrance door.

"How you gettin' home?" Mills asked.

"I guess I'll just catch a cab."

"You want me to take you home?"

"Evidently you wanna take me home." Farrah laughed.

"C'mon." Mills pushed himself off the wall.

As he walked toward the exit, Mills wondered if taking Farrah home was the right move. Since he'd known her, he'd always avoided being alone with her in fear of what his tongue and hands might do. So far, he hadn't done a good job hiding his true feelings for her. She was his pot'nah's girl. Sure, she and Khalil were broken up, but with their track record they'd be back together in no time.

Besides that, Mills had no business even thinking about Farrah in any other way than as a friend. But the more he was around her the more he found it harder to. She was drop-dead gorgeous inside and out. Her smile lit up an entire room and her warm personality made the shyest of people want to open up. Mills often kicked himself for not finding her first. But none of that mattered because she was off-limits.

Outside in the cool air Mills and Farrah walked to his silver Audi R8 while making small talk. Both were extremely nervous to be around the other without anyone there to stop them from acting on their lustful urges. Inside his car they jumped on Olive Street and headed toward Farrah's crib.

"I know you said you was cool but you sure you're a'ight?" Mills probed. "What happened between you and my man was pretty fucked up."

"I don't even wanna get into all that. My heart already feels like it got a fat chick sittin' on it."

Farrah looked out the window, determined not to think of Khalil.

"I can respect that." Mills chuckled. "I'd rather talk about how pretty you are anyway."

"Stop." Farrah laughed.

"What? You act like I'm lying or something."

"Whatever, Corey," Farrah said as they pulled up to her place.

"You're the only person I know who calls me by my first name. Why?"

"'Cause, if I called you Mills then I would be like everybody else and I'm not like everybody else."

"You're right about that." He looked at her out of the corner of his eye. "A'ight, then, li'l lady"—Mills placed the car into park—"it was good seeing you."

"You mean to tell me you not gon' walk me to the door?"

"Oh, my bad. I ain't know you wanted me to." Mills turned off the ignition and got out.

As they strolled up the walkway leading to Farrah's door, Farrah wondered if she should invite Mills in, but quickly nixed the idea.

"Well, thanks for bringing me home." She turned around and faced him once they approached her door.

"No problem. You know I'd do anything for you." Mills stared deep into her eyes.

"Good night, sir." She patted him on the arm, trying to keep things strictly platonic.

"Oh word?" Mills jerked his head back. "That's all I get is a pat on the arm? You betta give me a hug, girl." He pulled her into his embrace.

Farrah tried her hardest not to blush while wrapping her arms around Mills's waist. With her breasts pressed up against his firm chest, Mills engulfed the intoxicating smell of her perfume. It should've been against the law for him to be that close to her. The feel of Farrah's petite frame being in his arms was too much for him to handle.

And yes, his conscience was telling him to let her go and keep it moving, but the feelings he'd kept hidden for the last four years came pouring out onto the surface, and he found his lips upon hers.

Entrapped in his arms, Farrah rotated between sucking his top and bottom lip while thinking, *is this really happening?*

She'd secretly dreamed of this moment since the first day she'd laid eyes on Mills. Sometimes when she and Khalil made love she fantasized that he was Mills, and now that her fantasy was becoming her reality she never wanted the moment to end. Ready to take things to the next level, Mills slid his hand up Farrah's skirt and caressed her thighs. As Mills's fingers toyed with Farrah's clit regret swarmed his soul. Coming to his senses he abruptly ended the kiss. The taste of Farrah's sweet lips still lingered on his lips as he stepped back.

"What's wrong?" Farrah asked, running her tongue across her bottom lip.

"We can't be doing this." Mills gazed down at the ground, feeling guilty.

"Aww yeah, I forgot." She chuckled. "You got a girl."

Mills focused his attention on Farrah and stood silent. He did have a girl and they'd been together six years, so he had no business being at another woman's doorstep at 3:00 a.m., tonguing her down.

"Yeah, and I'm your man's friend so we most definitely need to fall all the way back."

"You're right." Farrah cleared her throat, becoming uncomfortable.

"I'ma shake." Mills pointed his head toward his car.

"Yeah, you should." Farrah looked at him.

"I'ma holla at you later." Mills placed his hands inside his pocket and walked away.

Floating on a cloud made of cotton candy, Farrah unlocked her door and stepped inside. She couldn't believe that she and Mills had shared a kiss. The moment was tantalizing and forbidden, causing the kiss to be even more electric than it already was. But they could never cross the line like that again. Too many people would get hurt if they acted on their emotions. And Farrah wasn't willing to add more drama to her life for anybody, not even Mills.

Chapter Three

Finally I can see you crystal clear.
—Adele, "Rolling In The Deep"

It was funny to Farrah how she could go from absolutely detesting the thought of being near Khalil to yearning for him every second of the day. This love thang was a tricky little bastard. Every other minute her emotions shifted. She went from hating Khalil to missing his touch every time the wind blew. And yes, she knew missing him was no good for anyone, especially her, but she hated being alone.

For four years she and Khalil spent every waking moment together. It'd been strange doing normal everyday activities without him. The first time she went to the market alone she felt lost. Every move she made she wished he were there to take with her. It was absurd how one person could impact her life so much.

Determined to get Khalil out of her mind, Farrah focused on her job. She and London owned and operated a styling and makeup company called the Glam Squad. In less than twenty-four hours they'd be in New York City styling R&B artist Teddy for a shoot with *Complex* magazine. She had to pick out the dopest clothes and accessories, so that afternoon she hit up stores like Avalon and R-Sole in the Delmar Loop. That very moment she was walking into a new store called Devil City that specialized in modern versions of fifties-style clothing. While picking up a pair of dark indigo blue slim-fit jeans her cell began to ring.

"Hello?" she answered.

"What you doing?" London asked.

"Grabbing a few more clothes for the shoot."

"I thought you were done."

"Nah. You can never have too many options." Farrah placed the jeans back on the rack.

"That's true."

"I think when we get to New York I'm going to pull some things from BBC."

"That would be hot. I figured out the look I wanna go for with the female model," London said, excited. "I'm going to go for an eighties glam sex goddess look. Very reminiscent of Blondie."

"Gorg," Farrah exclaimed.

"I know this is what I do," London complimented herself.

"You know we got to kill this shoot, right?" Farrah questioned.

"Please believe I do. This could put our company on the map," London agreed.

"We have to have everything on point. That means showing up on time, *London*." Farrah stressed her name.

"I know you ain't tryin' to read me," London responded.

"Oh, but I am."

"Whatever. You gettin' out tonight?"

"No! See this is what I'm talkin' about, London. Our flight leaves at four o'clock in the morning and you talkin' about going out," Farrah said, disappointed.

"Only for a minute, Farrah, damn! Quit being so damn uptight. You know, let me get off this phone, 'cause I already know where this conversation is heading. I'll see you when you get home." London hung up before Farrah could reply.

"Heffa." Farrah chuckled, hanging up too.

London was great at being a makeup artist but being on time for her appointments was not her forte, and her tardiness had cost them major business in the past. Farrah couldn't afford for London's unprofessionalism to ruin their biggest opportunity to date. They had to put their best foot forward and nail this shoot.

After pulling several items from Devil City, Farrah headed to her Jeep only to get the shock of her life. As soon as she stepped onto the sidewalk she spotted Khalil walking down the street. But he wasn't alone. A tall stick-figure woman, who looked like she'd just stepped off a Paris runway, was holding his hand.

Farrah's heart instantly dropped to her feet. Her eyes had to be deceiving her. No way could he be with someone already. They'd only been broken up two months. How could he already be giving to someone else what was supposed to be on reserve for her? Then their eyes met and instead of acknowledging her, Khalil turned his attention back to the girl and wrapped his arm around her neck, as if what they shared never existed.

Distraught, Farrah watched, unable to breathe until their backs faded into the afternoon sunlight. Choking back the tears that flooded her throat, Farrah rushed to her car and got in. Heavy, salty tears quickly cascaded down her cheeks as her head hit the headrest. From that moment on she vowed not to reminisce on old memories of Khalil, sniff the scent of cologne left in his shirts, or stare at pictures of him 'cause none of it mattered.

No matter how many good times they shared with one another he still was the one person in her life who constantly made her cry. And yes, Farrah knew the day would come when she'd see him with someone new, but she never imagined the ache in the center of her chest would be so excruciating. It was time for her to move on. Any feelings she still harbored for Khalil were going to be buried and burned. All she needed was a fire extinguisher to put out the never-ending flame.

The atmosphere inside the Tribeca studio was live. *Complex* magazine reps, the famed photographer Bruce Ervin and his staff, Teddy and his crew, as well as the Glam Squad were all in the building. Farrah watched with delight as Teddy stood in front of a white backdrop dressed in a Knicks hat, Louis Vuitton shades, black G-Star tank top, Mishka skinny-leg jeans, and Y-3 Yohji Yamamoto sneakers. It was one of his favorite looks of the day. So far he'd been extremely pleased with all of Farrah's choices.

The photographer loved London's eighties glam makeup look for the female model who accompanied Teddy on the shoot. Things couldn't have been going better. The editor-in-chief of *Complex* already wanted to work with Farrah and London again on another shoot in a few weeks.

"I got what I need for this setup," Bruce confirmed. "Farrah, let's try the leather jacket and jeans look next."

"Sure." She nodded, heading over to the rack of clothing she'd brought in.

"Ay. Guess what I just heard." London rushed over to Farrah with a concealor brush in her hand.

"What?"

"Yo' boy is in town and he's throwing a party at his crib tonight in Brooklyn."

"Who?"

"Mills." London grinned from ear to ear.

"That's what's up." Farrah tried to play it off like she didn't care, when really her heart fluttered at the sound of his name.

"Don't act like you don't wanna go," London teased.

"Yeah, you should come. Mills is my homeboy," Teddy said, taking off his shirt, revealing a six pack of muscle.

"Oh I'm 'cumming' all right." London licked her lips, causing Teddy to blush.

"Seriously, y'all should slide through. From what I heard it's gon' be off the chain," Teddy added.

"Oh, we'll be there." London shot him a sexy grin.

"No, you'll be there. I'll be in my hotel room, asleep," Farrah quipped.

After the awkward moment in front of her door she didn't want to risk coming off like a stalker by just showing up to Mills's spot unannounced. Plus, his chick would be there and her presence would only make things weirder.

"You are so lame, Farrah. Come on. Get the stick outta ya ass and have fun for a change. We're in fuckin' New York City for God's sake," London whined, stomping her foot.

"No." Farrah ignored her whining and handed Teddy his shirt.

"Pleaaaaaase," London pleaded. "You know I can't go by myself. He's your friend. Come on, Farrah. I promise we'll only stay for an hour or two." London poked out her bottom lip.

Caving in, Farrah said, "Okay, but we're only going to stay an hour."

"Or two." London smirked, skipping away.

***

Farrah didn't know what to expect when the freight elevator doors to Mills's $3.5 million warehouse/home opened, but she never in her wildest dreams thought her eyes would witness the kind of debauchery that was going on inside. It was as if she'd been transported into a world of hip hop hedonism. She was completely in awe.

N.E.R.D's infamous strip club anthem "Lapdance" set the mood upon entrance. A colorful array of strobe lights lit the place. Farrah had to strain her eyes in order not to run into anything or anyone. There was so much going on she couldn't concentrate. People were all over the place. Some were dancing, others were making out, skateboarding, taking body shots, playing beer pong, skinny dipping, or puffin' on la.

Since she'd walked in, she'd spotted numerous celebrities. Terry Kennedy, Fabolous, Jessie J, Big Sean, and Teyana Taylor were all in the building. As she and London searched the crowd for someone they personally knew, Farrah took in Mills's crib. His place had a gritty, eclectic feel to it.

It was so huge that he had an indoor skate ramp, basketball court, and pool. Graffiti paint and BUA paintings adorned the walls. An offbeat selection of furniture filled the space. One room in particular was decorated with nothing but one-of-a-kind sneakers. Another room held all of Mills's custom-made bikes on the ceiling and walls.

On top of the quirky décor and untamed atmosphere, Farrah quickly realized that she was overdressed. She'd worn the tightest dress and tallest heels she could find. The black, one-shoulder mini dress with a cutout side and gold sequin arm hit the middle of her thighs highlighting the five-inch Ruthie Davis double platform peep-toe pumps with multi-studded straps. Everyone else besides London, who also wore a freakum dress, was dressed in T-shirts, shorts, and jeans. She and London stuck out like sore thumbs.

"I knew I should'a stayed my ass back at the hotel," she hissed.

"Oh, hush. It's better to be overdressed than underdressed." London flipped her hair and smiled at a guy walking by.

"Whore," Farrah spat out of the side of her mouth.

"Cross-eyed cow," London spat back.

"Y'all came?" Teddy approached them both with a hug.

"I sure did." London bit her bottom lip, look-ing him up and down.

"You a li'l nasty girl ain't you?" Teddy asked.

"What?" London cocked her head back. "You ain't know? As a matter of fact how would you like to live underneath my skirt?"

"As long as you got a bikini wax. I like a clean work space," he flirted back.

"Well, we all good to go then," London confirmed.

"Come take a walk wit' me." Teddy took London by the hand.

"Toodles." She waved her hand over her shoulder to Farrah.

I can't believe this bitch just left me standing here, Farrah thought, rolling her eyes. *I could'a been back at the room eating room service.* Thirsty, Farrah walked over to the open bar and ordered an apple martini. With her drink in her hand she turned and faced the crowd. Everyone was having such a good time except her. She felt like at any moment she would cry.

The loneliness that plagued her was all too consuming. She hated that no matter what she did or who she was with she couldn't find joy. She was starting to wonder if she would ever feel pure happiness again or if she ever had. Figuring she'd finish her drink and leave, Farrah took a sip from her glass when she noticed Mills standing across the room. He was surrounded by his pot'nahs, but even in their midst he stood out the most.

Mills's swagger was off the charts. The sky-blue sweatshirt with three hot pink ice cream cones on the front, yellow G-Shock watch, khaki cargo shorts, and Space Jam Jordans enhanced his looks to another level of fineness. Farrah realized it was wrong to lust over him but she couldn't help herself. All she could imagine was him lifting her up into the air and her wrapping her legs around his back as he carried her to his bedroom.

As the DJ began to slow it down by playing Cee Lo Green's "Bodies" and Cee Lo sang the words, "Sweetheart this won't hurt a bit . . . I can kill it wit' kindness or murder it," Mills turned his head and noticed her staring at him. Immediately a smile graced the corners of his lips. Over the loud chatter and drum kick from the beat the two inched toward one another slowly.

Mills couldn't take his eyes off the curves of her frame. The dress clung to her body so tight he could see the imprint of her hard nipples through the fabric. Face-to-face he reached down and wrapped his arms snuggly around her waist.

"What you doing here?" he asked letting her go.

"I styled Teddy today for a photo shoot and he told me about the party. It's not a problem that I'm here right?"

"Nah, you know better than that," Mills assured her. "How long you gon' be in town?"

"Until Sunday, you?"

"Damn I'm leaving Sunday too," he replied, surprised.

"You know this is quite a crowd you got here." Farrah looked around nervously.

"I know. I had to break the place in."

"Where is Jade?" Farrah referred to his girlfriend. "I don't see her."

"Back in St. Louis. She couldn't make it," Mills lied.

He was too embarrassed to tell Farrah that his girlfriend had opted not to come. Lately she'd been acting distant and giving him nothin' but attitude. Since he'd been in New York he'd called her over ten times and she hadn't answered the phone but once.

"I wanted to apologize to you for what happened when I brought you home that night. I was way out of line," he said sincerely.

"No apologies necessary," Farrah pledged. "It takes two to tango. Khalil is your friend and Jade is your girl. We wouldn't want to do anything that might jeopardize that, right?" She arched her eyebrow.

"Right." Mills nodded his head, knowing damn well if neither person existed he'd take it there with her in a heartbeat.

"But uh anyway let me introduce you to my peoples." Mills led her across the room by the hand.

The touch of his soft skin on hers almost caused Farrah to faint. Being strictly his friend was turning out to be far more difficult than she'd anticipated. In order to keep her feelings in check, Farrah remembered that anything besides a friendship for them would be life threatening. So she placed her feelings for him aside and allowed herself to enjoy Mills's company as a friend and nothing more.

Chapter Four

You're actin' like you can't make no time for me.
—Brandy, "How I Feel"

Just take a deep breath and breathe. You don't have anything to lose. The only thing he can say is, "I don't wanna be wit' you," Jade thought as she sat inside Lambert Airport awaiting her homie/lover/friend Rock's arrival from L.A. They'd been seeing each other sporadically for the past eight months. Jade would never forget the day they met.

She was at Diddy's annual white party in the Hamptons when she sashayed across the lawn in her six-inch Manolos and her heel got stuck. Embarrassed beyond belief she kneeled down to pull her heel from the grass when Rock, being the gentleman he was, came over to help.

"You good?" he asked in a deep tone.

"I got it," Jade said with an attitude, rolling her eyes.

She was not in the mood for another wannabe rapper or tired ballplayer hitting on her. But when she looked up and locked eyes with his, her heart skipped a beat. She'd seen pictures of him in magazines such as *Vibe*, *XXL*, and *GQ* but none of the photos did his looks any justice. He was beautiful, deliciously delectable to be exact. She'd never seen anything like him.

Rock was six foot and 190 pounds. His warm brown skin, spinning waves, almond-shaped eyes, goatee, and sexy, full lips made her mouth water. Rock's body was ripped to say the least from years of being a professional basketball player. And the treasure chest of tattoos all over his body made her want him even more.

Before him, Jade never imagined herself catching feelings for another man. She loved Mills but things between them had become mundane. The newness of their relationship had long since worn off. There was no spark. They'd gone to the same places, did it in every position imaginable more than twice, shared every secret there was to share, and argued over everything under the sun.

She knew him inside and out. He was her best friend, but Jade craved more than a man who adored her and showered her with material things. She craved adventure and Rock gave her exactly what she wanted. He ignited a flame inside her that hadn't been lit in years. He made her feel alive again, sexy, and naughty.

With him everything was a mystery. He never gave her too much of himself, just enough to keep her wanting more and she loved it. And the sex was mind blowing. They'd done it everywhere: the movie theater, the park after dark, and public restrooms. Their love affair was off the hook. Either she went to see him or vice versa. Jade didn't even care to be discreet. Whenever Rock called she came running.

Now here she was pushing herself to do the unthinkable. She was over keeping her feelings for him bottled up inside. She wanted more. She wanted to be his woman. She was done with him treating her like his girl without officially giving her the title. It was time for them to put everything on the line and see where this road they were on was headed. *Okay, here he comes,* she thought as his plane landed and passengers started to depart. Jade stood up in anticipation of seeing his face.

Her heart was beating a mile a minute. She hoped like hell he liked the way she looked. Jade was always secure with her appearance because she was drop-dead gorgeous, but with Rock she always felt the need to be on point. No matter where she was Jade always stood out in the crowd. Her blond buzz cut like Amber Rose complemented her creamy butter-colored skin perfectly. Jade's angelic almond-shaped eyes, button nose, and pink heart-shaped lips were a far contrast to her sinful physique.

She was five-foot-eight and had a body that put most video vixens to shame. Her measurements rounded out to be a perfect 34-24-38. Homegirl had breasts, hips, and ass for days, and the giant rose tattoo on her right shoulder gave her an even more edgy appeal.

Jade couldn't wait to surprise Rock with the custom-designed necklace she had designed for him. And although his resume was impressive how fat his pockets were didn't faze Jade a bit. She loved his energy, his ambition, and most importantly his heart.

Smiling from ear to ear, Jade watched closely as the passengers from Rock's flight filed into the airport. After a few minutes she realized that everyone had exited and that Rock wasn't anywhere to be found. Perplexed, she walked over to the ticket agent.

"Excuse me. Was there a Tyrin Rhodes on this flight?"

"I'm sorry, ma'am, but we can't divulge that kind of information," the ticket agent informed her.

Becoming angry, Jade turned around and stood helplessly. She couldn't figure out where in the hell Rock was. She'd just spoken to him before he headed to the airport and he'd confirmed that he was coming. Then out of the corner of her eye she spotted him. There he was standing in the middle of the corridor with his back facing her. Beaming from the inside out, Jade rushed over to him. It would've broken her heart if he hadn't showed up like he'd done so many times before.

"Here I am, baby." She wrapped her arms around his neck and kissed his cheek.

"Excuse me?" The guy she assumed was Rock turned around.

Shocked to find that it wasn't him, Jade's face burned bright red.

"I am so sorry," she pleaded, stepping back.

Embarrassed beyond belief she walked away in a rush. She'd never been so humiliated in her life. Standing next to a water fountain she gathered her emotions and called Rock.

"Hello?" A woman answered the phone.

"Umm." Jade took the phone away from ear and looked at the screen to ensure she'd dialed the right number. Seeing that she had she asked, "May I speak to Rock?"

"Yeah, hold on. Tyrin, telephone!" the woman yelled.

Seconds later he got on the phone. "What up?"

"Hey," Jade said, slightly perturbed. "Where are you? I'm standing in the airport lookin' for you."

"Yo, my bad. I forgot to call you and tell you I wasn't coming."

"Say that again?" Jade's heart dropped.

"I'm not gon' make it. My son got a game today. C'mon, TJ!" he yelled, clapping his hands.

"So that was your son's mother who answered the phone?" Jade probed.

"Yeah, we at the game now."

Jade let out a surprised chuckle. She knew Rock wasn't her man, but the fact that he was not only with his ex-wife but allowed her to answer his phone fucked her up.

"Wow," she replied, feeling stupid.

"What's wrong wit' you?"

"Nothin'," Jade lied.

"Yes, it is. What, you mad?" Rock asked in a low tone.

"What the fuck you think?" Jade spat back sarcastically. "Of course I'm mad! You got me standing in the airport lookin' a goddamn fool!"

"Ay yo, babe! Bring me back a water!" Rock shouted, completely ignoring her.

"Who the fuck are you callin' babe?" Jade snapped.

"Mya."

"Who the hell is Mya?" Jade screwed up her face.

"You know who Mya is. That's my son's mother."

"Oh, word? So y'all on them kind of speaking terms. You callin' her babe and shit."

"You buggin'."

"I'm buggin'?" Jade said in disbelief.

"Yeah, and where you at anyway? You at home?"

"Nigga, are you conscious? I'm at the airport waitin' on yo' black ass! You know what?" Jade checked herself. "I ain't got time for this shit! You and yo' fuckin' son's mother go be a family together!" She hung up the phone, heated.

Seconds later Rock called her back.

"What?" she answered on the first ring.

"C'mon, Blondie, don't be like that." Rock called her by the nickname he'd given her, causing her to soften a bit.

"Nah, I'm tired of this shit." She sighed, massaging her forehead.

"I know and I'm sorry. You were right. I was wrong. I forgot. I should'a called but you know I don't get to see my son as much I would like to since I'm always traveling."

"Mmm, hmm." Jade rolled her eyes.

"I swear to God I got you," he promised.

"Yeah, whatever, Tyrin."

"Oh, you must really be mad. You callin' me by my first name." Rock chuckled.

"Ain't nothin' funny. I really was lookin' forward to seeing you." Jade looked down at the gift she held in her hand.

"I wanted to see you too." He spoke softly.

"Daddy, did you see me? I made a homerun!" Jade heard his six-year-old son, TJ, say in the background.

"Look, go ahead, handle that. I'll just talk to you later," she said, annoyed.

"A'ight," Rock replied reluctantly before hanging up.

Picking her shattered heart off the floor Jade headed toward the exit door. *I don't even see why I bother,* she thought walking to her car. She hated that she allowed herself to get amped up over spending time with him. Rock wasn't even her man.

She had a man so their so-called "relationship" could never work. At that moment Jade realized she'd been playing herself. She and Rock were never going to be anything more than friends with benefits, so it was best she fell back. She couldn't continue to make herself readily available every time he called.

Jade chirped the alarm on her black Porsche Boxster and made the sunroof go back. Fed up, she threw the box with the necklace inside it into the back seat and hopped in, when her cell phone began to ring. It was Mills. Not in the mood to talk to him she sent his call to voice mail. She didn't feel like him giving her a guilt trip about not coming to New York.

When it came down to spending time with him or Rock there was no question of who she was choosing. Rock won hands down. But now that he'd played her she started to wonder if she had made the wrong decision.

Mills gazed absently out of the window while holding his phone in his hand. He and Farrah were at Cafeteria in New York having lunch but he couldn't get his mind off of Jade. He'd just tried calling her again and once more she'd opted not to answer. For months he'd tried pinpointing exactly when and where things between them went wrong. But for the life of him he couldn't remember the space and time.

It was like one day he woke up and she'd changed. If he breathed too loud she was annoyed, and when they made love it seemed as if she was physically there but mentally somewhere else. He'd contemplated walking away, but after six years of being together he thought their relationship was worth the fight. Hell, he loved her and at some point wanted to marry her.

Farrah gazed across the table and looked at Mills. They'd spent the last two days with one another. They'd gone shopping and seen the play *Fela!* on Broadway, but the fake smile that Mills plastered on his face didn't fool Farrah one bit. There was no denying the pain that lay behind his brown eyes.

She knew that look like she knew a knockoff handbag because since her and Khalil's breakup she'd had the same expression on her face. Normally she didn't pry into her friends' personal lives, but over the years Mills had become somewhat of a confidant during her and Khalil's trying times. He'd stayed neutral while letting her know that her happiness was what mattered most. Now it was time for Farrah to return the favor. She just hoped that she could keep her feelings for him out of the equation.

"What's wrong?" She leaned her elbows on the table.

"Huh?" Mills blinked his eyes, coming out of a trance.

"What's wrong wit' you? It seems to me like you're upset about something."

"Man." Mills sighed. "Jade on some bullshit."

"What she do?"

"We was supposed to come to New York this week for a vacation and at the last minute she flipped and said she wasn't coming." He screwed up his face.

"Why?" Farrah asked.

"When you find out let me know," Mills said sarcastically.

"Have you talked to her?"

"I called but she won't answer."

"You text her?" Farrah quizzed.

"Farrah, I've done it all," he stressed. "I've texted her, left her voice mail messages. She just won't hit me back."

"You think something could've happened to her?"

"The fucked-up part about it is"—Mills chuckled—"her ass can't answer my calls but she can post shit on Facebook and Twitter."

"Wow. Homegirl off the chain," Farrah said, stunned.

"Who you tellin'? I'm tryin' to give her the benefit of the doubt but she got me fucked up."

"Have y'all been having problems?"

"I wasn't trippin' off it at first but now it seems like all we do is argue over silly shit. Every time I turn around she got an attitude about something. And when I try to talk to her about it and see what's up she come at me like I'm gettin' on her nerves. So I just been like fuck it." Mills sat back in his chair and shrugged his shoulders.

"Y'all just goin' through a rough patch. Everything will be a'ight." Farrah tried to seem optimistic.

"I hope so." Mills shook his head.

Farrah wished she could make all of his frustration and pain go away. Jade was a complete and utter fool for treating a man like Mills the way she did. Women all over the world, including her, would die for the chance to be his girl. And yes, there were always two sides to every story, but after knowing and being around Mills she'd never seen or heard of him being a dog.

A million-dollar man deserved a million-dollar bitch, and if Jade didn't step up to the plate and handle her business another woman gladly would. And Farrah was just the woman to do it.

"Mmm." Farrah gazed down at her cell phone and rolled her eyes.

"What?" Mills asked, taking a small sip of his drink.

"It's Khalil." Farrah picked up her phone and pressed answer. "Hello?"

"Hey," he said.

"Hi," Farrah replied dryly. Her heart was beating out of her chest to the point she couldn't breathe.

"Ay, is it all right if I come by and get the rest of my things tomorrow?" Khalil asked with an attitude.

"No. I'm out of town but I'll be back Sunday. So if you wanna come by after then you're more than welcome," she said sweetly, knowing it would aggravate the shit outta him.

"A'ight, well, I'll be over there Monday around two. Is that cool?"

"Yeah."

"A'ight then," Khalil replied before hanging up.

Farrah took the phone away from her ear and inhaled deeply.

"What he say?" Mills questioned as soon as she hung up.

"He's finally coming to get his stuff."

"You should be happy." Mills eyed her quizzically. He noticed that she was upset. "I mean that's my homeboy and all but you got too much going for yourself to be letting someone treat you bad. Any man would be lucky to have you. You got your shit together."

"I so don't have it together." Farrah played with her food. "I'm the girl who'll friend your mother on Facebook and start showing up to events I wasn't invited to." She cracked up laughing.

"Shut up." Mills chuckled, throwing his napkin at her.

"Seriously . . . I'm happy." Farrah forced a smile onto her face. "Khalil will finally be outta my life for good now." She swallowed hard.

In a matter of days the door to her and Khalil's relationship would be closed. Farrah thought that she was ready and prepared for it, but now that the moment was approaching she was secretly hesitant to end it. What if she was making a mistake? What if Khalil was able to change and be the man she always dreamed he could be?

Then Farrah kept in mind that she'd asked God on more than one occasion for discernment over the situation, and since then Khalil hadn't helped her with the rent, repaid her for the things he'd destroyed, or apologized. Being the moocher he was he'd already found a new woman to lie up under, so maybe losing him wasn't a bad thing after all, but a blessing in disguise.

Chapter Five

Jade stood in front of the mirror at The
Twisted Olive, applying another coat of red
Chanel lipstick, when her cell phone began to
ring. By the ringtone she knew it was Rock.
Standing perfectly still she wondered if she
should even answer. She hadn't fully prepared
the slick shit she was going to hit him with when
they spoke again.

Besides that, she was having a good time and
didn't feel like Rock altering her mood. Plus, it
would be good if she gave him a dose of his own
medicine and didn't pick up the phone. Rock
needed to know how it felt to wait by the phone
and wonder what she was doing and who she
was with. But Jade was digging Rock far too

much to play childish games with him. Her ears were yearning to hear the sound of his deep voice so she answered on the fourth ring.

"Hello?" she answered with a slight giggle. She had to let him know that she was out having a good time and not sitting at home waiting for him to call.

"Where you at?" he asked with an attitude.

"Who is this?" Jade replied, trying her best not to laugh.

"Really, Jade?" Rock said mockingly.

"Oh," Jade responded dryly. "What's up?"

"Where you at?" he asked her again.

"Why?"

"Yo, let's stop this right now. Either you gon' tell me where you at or I'ma hang up. I'm tired. I ain't got time to be playin' a bunch of games. I just caught the fuckin' red eye out here just to see you."

"You're in St. Louis?" Jade's heart skipped a beat.

"Yeah, so you can dead your attitude 'cause I'm tryin' to see you."

A huge smile spread across Jade's face. She was overjoyed that he cared enough to cut his time with his son just to make her happy.

"I'm at The Twisted Olive," she finally replied.

"I'm like two minutes away so be outside when I get there." Rock hung up before she could reply.

"Cocky bastard." She tossed her phone back into her purse and headed toward the door.

Outside of the club she spotted Rock sitting on the hood of his black Ferrari. The stars from up above seemed to shine down on his face. As she walked toward him, Jade tried coming up with all kind of reasons to make her heart believe that Rock wasn't the one for her, but she couldn't find any. No other man had this effect on her. Not even Mills. The veins inside her body yearned for him.

Rock cocked his head to the side and eyed every inch of Jade's frame. Babygirl was hazardous to his health. He'd come across a lot of beautiful women in his life but none held a candle to her. Everything from her innocent eyes to her rose tattoo was spellbinding. It was hard for him to control himself when he was next to her.

And no, with her it wasn't just a physical thing. Jade's no-nonsense attitude, upbeat personality, sarcastic wit, drive to succeed, and unwavering devotion to him made him dig her even more. She was the truth and although Rock wasn't her man what they shared was a sure thing. With her arms folded across her chest, Jade stood in front of Rock and shot him a look that could kill.

"Hi," she said with a roll of the eyes.

"Keep it up and yo' eyes gon' get stuck." Rock chuckled, pulling her in between his legs.

"I'm not laughin'." Jade tuned up her face.

"You can stop with the attitude now. I already let you get yo' shit off when you went off on me for not showing up."

"What's that's suppose to mean?" Jade's upper lip curled.

"It means I'm sorry so when you gon' forgive me?" Rock stroked her arms.

"I don't know." Jade shrugged her shoulders.

"C'mon, Blondie, a nigga tired. All I wanna do is go back to the crib and chill out wit' you. Can we do that, please? I miss you. I know you miss me too."

Instead of loosening up, Jade rolled her eyes again and crossed her arms.

"You just ain't gon' act right are you?" Rock unfolded her arms.

"No." Jade smiled slightly.

"Go 'head and smile. You know you want to." Rock wrapped her up in his arms and kissed her cheek.

"I most certainly will not." Jade erupted in laughter as he tickled the side of her stomach.

"That's my girl." He kissed her again.

Over being upset, Jade gave in and hugged Rock back. She couldn't pass up the opportunity to feel him in her arms.

"I missed you," she finally confessed, becoming lost in his touch.

"I missed you too." Rock held her hand and stood up. "C'mon. Let's go."

Jade lay on her back fully naked, watching with hunger in her eyes as Rock slid his dick back and forth between her titties. She wanted to lick it so bad but Rock wouldn't let her. He just kept on her teasing her.

"Mmm just like that," she moaned, pressing her breasts together. "Your fuckin' dick feels so good."

Rock grabbed the back of her head and groaned. He loved that Jade was a superfreak. Homegirl was down for just about anything. Sex with her was always an adventure.

"Oooooh you're so fuckin' hard," Jade said like a porn star. "You're so fuckin' hard!"

"You like that don't you?"

"Uh huh." She nodded. "I wanna suck it daddy!"

"No, I want you to ride it. You wanna ride this dick?" Rock removed his dick from between her breasts and massaged himself.

"Yeah," Jade said fervently and straddled him backward. Feverishly she inserted him inside her pussy and Rock began to pound her hard.

"Ahhhhh! Ahh! Yes! Fuck yes!" Jade groaned, licking her fingers then massaging her clit. "Yes . . . Yes . . . Yes . . . Yes!" She rotated her wet fingers round and round.

From behind Rock thoroughly enjoyed the view of her fat ass bouncing up and down on his dick. The sight alone made him want to cum. But he didn't want to cum while she was riding him. Rock had to take control of the situation. In a matter of seconds Jade was on her back again with one leg sprawled over his shoulder.

"Aww yeah." She rolled her hip.

"You like that big dick don't you?" Rock smacked one of her titties.

"I love your cock!" Jade felt herself cumming. "You gon' cum on my titties?" she yelled. "Cum on my titties, daddy," she begged, cumming.

Rock couldn't hold it anymore. The nut in the tip of his dick was dying to come out. Quickly pulling out he did exactly what he was told and nutted all over Jade's breasts. After coming down from their orgasmic high Jade turned and looked at Rock.

"Damn that was good," she panted, pulling the cover up over her bottom half.

"You want some water?" Rock got out of the bed and headed down the stairs.

"Yeah." She wiped sweat from her forehead.

Jade wished she felt guilty about fuckin' her side nigga in the bed she shared with her man but she didn't. As far as Rock knew the loft she lived in was hers. He had no idea that he was smashin' her in the place she shared with Mills. And by the time Mills returned home Rock would be long gone so she was good.

"Where the cups at?" Rock yelled from the kitchen.

"In the cabinet on the right!" Jade yelled back as her cell began to ring. It was Mills calling her for the umpteenth time. Doing as she'd done all week long she sent his call to voice mail.

Seconds later Rock returned with two glasses of ice cold water. "You know as soon as I get back in that bed I'ma be knocked out." He handed her her glass.

"Oh, I know. After that nut you just busted you should be asleep until next week." Jade laughed, taking a sip of water. "Before you get back in bed, can you hand me a towel please?" she asked.

Rock reached into the linen closet and threw her a face towel. Jade carefully wiped the cum off her chest.

"Soooooo." She placed the towel down on the nightstand by the bed.

Since they'd linked up outside of the club she'd contemplated when the perfect time would be to bring up Rock's baby mama situation. Everything between them was going good and she didn't want to rock the boat. But she had to ask or else the what-if's in her mind would eat her up inside.

"So what?" Rock jumped back into bed and lay on top of her. "What's on yo' mind, Blondie? You got that look in yo' eye."

"I just wanted to know what's the deal between you and yo' son's mother?"

"I told you we cool." He kissed both of her cheeks.

"Yeah, but how cool? Do y'all still mess around?" Jade probed.

"Nah, it even nothin' like that."

"Then what is it like if you don't mind me askin'?"

"Actually I do," Rock replied, rolling over onto his back, obviously annoyed. "I thought we had an understanding that we do what we do," he continued.

"And we do. I just—"

"Look," Rock cut her off. "Let's not complicate things by questioning one another. I don't ask you nothin' about yo' nigga."

"What that got to do wit' anything?" Jade looked at him sideways.

"I mean I'm here wit' you ain't I? That's all that matters. Anything else ain't even worth talkin' about," Rock explained.

"But to me it is," Jade replied, not letting up.

"Why though?" Rock shrugged his shoulders. "We just friends, right?"

Hit with the reality of their agreement and that Rock clearly didn't want it to change, Jade quickly checked herself. *I am puttin' way too much energy into this nigga. If he wanna just be friends that's exactly what we're gon' be. Hell I got a man anyway.*

"You sholl right." She smirked. There was no way she was giving him the chain she bought now.

"Just come lie down." He pulled her close to him.

Rock knew that he'd been a little short with her, but he had to keep things between them in perspective. He'd already given his heart to a woman only to have it broken in a million pieces. After divorcing Mya he vowed to never give himself emotionally to a woman again. For the first time in a long time he was happy and sure Jade was a phenomenal woman but Rock wasn't trying to be tied down. If they'd met at a different time and space in his life maybe he would've wifed her but unfortunately for her being in a relationship wasn't in the cards for Rock. His main focus was his son and maintaining a successful basketball career. Anything besides that didn't matter, and if Jade couldn't understand that then she would have to be exed out of his life for good.

Days later, Mills stormed into his crib on a mission to kill. The two-hour flight from New York to St. Louis seemed to last forever. The entire plane ride all he did was envision himself confronting Jade. Now the moment had arrived. He'd finally get the answers he'd been searching for all week. The sun was setting as he barged into his bedroom and found Jade sitting in front of her vanity mirror, applying her makeup while listening to her iPod. Homegirl looked as if she didn't have a care in the world, pissing Mills off even more.

"Jade!" He placed his hand on her shoulder, causing her to jump.

"Damn, boy, you scared the shit outta me." She held her chest with her hand.

Mills took the earphones from her ears and said, "Why the fuck haven't you been answering my calls?"

"Well hi to you too, Mills." She rolled her eyes.

"You can stop wit' the bullshit. Answer the question," he demanded.

"What question?" Jade said coyly.

Mills licked his upper lip, trying his best not to explode.

"You know damn well you heard me the first time. On some real shit, Jade." Mills pointed his finger at her. "You pushin' it. You know I'm tryin' to be cool. I'm tryin' to work it out wit' you. But you being mad disrespectful. I've been callin' you all fuckin' week and you been ignoring me. But you got the nerve to be all on Facebook and Twitter posting a bunch of dumb shit like I won't come home and bust yo' ass." He got in her face. "What the fuck kinda shit is that? If I would'a did you like that you and yo' li'l wack-ass girlfriends would'a been callin' me a lousy no-good-ass nigga."

"I don't know what you want me to say. I didn't feel like talkin'." Jade quickly shot up nervously.

She'd spotted a pair of Rock's boxer briefs on the floor. *This nigga must be tryin' to get me killed. I asked his ass when he left this morning if he'd packed everything,* she thought.

"What the fuck you mean you ain't feel like talkin'?" Mills watched her walk across the room.

"Exactly what I said." Jade spun around, blocking his view of the underwear. "When you left we was into it so what makes you think I wanted to spend the rest of the week arguing wit' you?"

"We was into it 'cause you got into yo' feelings for no damn reason and decided you didn't wanna to go to New York!" Mills shot back, heading to the bathroom. He had to take a piss.

"And I didn't wanna go and have you ignore me all week!" Jade hurried and picked up the underwear and threw them into her closet.

"Bullshit!" Mills flushed the toilet. "The whole reason I planned the trip was so we could spend some time together and you know it. So find a better excuse." He began washing his hands.

"I ain't gotta find shit! I already know what it is," Jade scoffed.

"Oh, word?" Mills came from out the bathroom and looked at her. "Well let me in on the secret so I can know what I need to do."

"Whatever, Mills." Jade flicked her wrist dismissively.

"And where the fuck you think you going?" he asked as she placed on her heels. "It's Sunday!"

"Out!" Jade stood in front of their full-length mirror and examined her outfit.

She was rockin' the hell out of a gray long-sleeved midriff-bearing top, tribal-print leggings, and five-inch DSquared ankle strap heels. The leggings she wore made her ass look like a watermelon. Despite how mad he was Mills tried his best to resist the temptation to want to fuck the shit outta her. Jade had all the right weaponry but her attitude sucked!

"We ain't seen each other all week. You really gettin' ready to go out?" Mills said, shocked.

"What you want me to do sit here and argue wit' you all night? I don't think so." Jade stacked two gold bracelets onto her wrist.

"Ain't nobody tryin' to argue wit' you. I'm just tryin' to see what's good wit' you."

For the first time since he'd returned home Jade allowed herself to see the distress written on Mills's face. It wasn't fair how she was treating him, but what was she to do when every fiber of her being yearned for another man? She still loved Mills and genuinely enjoyed his company. But the love she had for him over the years had become more of a friendship-type love.

Nothing about him was exciting or new. She knew what he would do and say sometimes before he did it. That still didn't give her the right to treat him like a stepchild because she couldn't keep what mattered most in her life in perspective. Then Rock's words popped into her brain. *We're just friends right?* Although she harbored deep feelings for him she couldn't let a side piece of dick outweigh six years of a solid relationship.

"Baby, I'm sorry." Jade walked up to Mills and batted her long eyelashes. "You're right, I should've answered your calls. I was wrong, and to be honest wit' you, I wish I would've gone to New York with you instead of staying here. I love you." She wrapped her arms around his neck. "And I know that things between us haven't been good lately but I promise that from this day forward I'ma put all of my energy into making sure we're straight."

"What you gon' do?" Mills caressed her ass.

"For starters"—Jade slowly dropped down low—"this." She unzipped his jeans.

Jade figured she'd suck his dick like a porn star in order to distract him from the fact that she wasn't going to give him any ass. During Rock's visit she'd fucked him so much her pussy was sore. Mills would instantly know the difference if she gave it up to him right then and there.

"You like that, baby?" she asked, sliding his dick all the way to the back of her throat, then pulling out.

"Hell, yeah." Mills closed his eyes, enjoying the sensation of her wet tongue.

Jade's plan was working. Ten minutes later Mills came long and hard in her mouth and to prove that she was dedicated to him and their relationship she swallowed every last drop.

Chapter Six

**Can't nobody tell me this is love when
you're immune to all my pain.**
—Beyoncé, "I Care"

Farrah couldn't keep still. It was 4:45 p.m.
and Khalil would be arriving any minute. She'd
checked her hair, light makeup, and body-hug-
ging outfit, fluffed the pillows, and dusted at least
five times. She had to make sure that everything
was perfect when he arrived. She wanted him
to see that without him her life had been better
than ever, although that wasn't entirely true.

Career-wise she'd been doing phenomenally,
but emotionally she was drowning. Most days it
seemed as if her head was barely above water. But
maybe now that Khalil was finally putting an end
to their never-ending story of drama she could
come up for air. Hearing the startling sound of
the doorbell ringing, Farrah took a much-needed
breath and walked down the steps. With her

hand on the knob, Farrah prepared herself for the worst and opened the door.

"What up?" Khalil gazed down at her.

The sight of his face brought back every emotion Farrah kept bottled up since she saw him in the Delmar Loop. She couldn't figure out if she wanted to slap him or fuck him. Despite his horrible ways she couldn't deny how physically attracted she was to him. Khalil's spellbinding good looks were one of the reasons she stayed with him so long.

"I put your stuff by the steps so you wouldn't have to go up and down both flights of steps." She stepped to the side to let him in.

"Good lookin' out," Khalil replied, walking up the stairs. Once he reached the second floor Khalil gazed around in awe. "Damn I ain't been in this muthafucka in a minute." Although he'd lived there for over two years to him it felt like he was in foreign territory. "Let me get started," Khalil said, picking up a box of his clothes.

For almost a half hour Farrah sat on the couch and watched as Khalil took his things out to his car one by one. With each trip to his car she felt her chest tighten. They'd been over for two months, but secretly she thought they'd get back together like the many times they had before. And, sure, she'd broken up with him, but she did it with the hope that he'd finally see all of the turmoil he'd put her through and change.

She thought that after being apart from her for a while he would realize all of the things she did for him and come running back on bended knee begging for forgiveness, but he didn't. Breaking up with him only proved how much of a dick Khalil really was. Now she realized how stupid she was for staying with him so long.

"This is the last of it," he announced, bringing her back to reality.

"Okay." Farrah stood up as Khalil began to walk down the steps with the last box.

"So that's it?" she belted out.

"What?" Khalil took a step backward and looked at her.

Farrah stood speechless; she hadn't even recognized she'd said anything until Khalil responded.

"Uhhhhh . . . I just wanna know is that it?" she repeated, feeling as if she was about to pass out.

"Is what it?" Khalil eyed her, perplexed.

"You just gon' leave and not say nothin'?"

"I mean . . . what you want me to say?" he responded nonchalantly.

"For starters how about 'I'm sorry.'"

"What am I apologizing to you for?" Khalil screwed up his face. "You broke up wit' me."

"Because you put my heart in the bottom of your shoe and stepped on it constantly, that's why!" Farrah felt her temperature rise. "For four years all you did was lie to me! You haven't helped me with the bills or the rent since I don't when—"

"Here we go wit' that shit again." Khalil rolled his eyes while putting down the box. "I didn't hear yo' ass complainin' when I was buying you Chanel bags and shit!"

"Khalil, you think 'cause you bought me a couple of bags and some clothes that that means something to me? None of that shit matters when you're constantly being lied to and abused!"

"Now I abused you?" He hung his head low and laughed.

"Are you fuckin' insane? Do you not remember all of the shit you did to me?"

"Whatever. I ain't come over here for this bullshit." Khalil bent back down to pick up the box.

"So are you gon' help me with the rent or what?" Farrah placed her hand on her hip.

"Are you conscious?" Khalil stood up straight. "What the fuck I look like helping you pay the rent when I don't live here anymore? You out yo' fuckin' mind."

"'Cause your name is on the lease, asshole," Farrah shouted, boiling with anger.

"Farrah, you broke up wit' me. What the fuck you mad for? If I'm such a horrible person then you should be happy I'm gone," Khalil yelled. "You can't be mad 'cause you broke up wit' me and now shit ain't going the way you wanted it to!"

"Correction," Farrah snapped, getting in his face. "I'm mad 'cause you haven't even said 'I'm sorry' for fuckin' up my shit. I'm mad because I wanted you to be fuckin' responsible. I'm mad because I wanted you to tell the truth for once in your life, among other things. That's why I'm mad, nigga! Don't get it twisted." She pointed her finger at him. "I gave you four years of my life, Khalil!" She stomped her foot, beginning to cry. "I ignored everything in me to be wit' you. Only for you to shit all over it. I took care of yo' black ass when you didn't have a pot to piss in. Your own family doesn't even wanna have nothin' to do with you. Hell, I should've dropped yo' ass when yo' mama said you wasn't shit."

"Unless you want me to crack yo' fuckin' skull in I suggest you not bring up my mother," Khalil warned, seething with anger.

"Oh, the truth hurts doesn't it?" Farrah rolled her neck and crossed her arms over her chest.

"Are you done 'cause I'm about to head out," Khalil replied, bored with the conversation.

"And you're really not gonna say you're sorry?" Farrah stood stunned as tears poured down her cheeks.

"No . . . I'm not." Khalil picked up the box.

"Okay." Farrah nodded her head profusely.

"I'm up." Khalil ignored her tears and walked down the steps.

Distraught, Farrah slowly strolled over to the middle of the living room floor, when the sound of the front door slamming shut caused her to jump.

"How can he be so fuckin' cruel?" she cried hysterically. "He doesn't even care. He doesn't even care." She cried so hard her chest heaved up and down.

"Fuck this." She swiftly wiped her eyes and grabbed her keys and purse.

After a ten-minute drive Farrah parked her car and sauntered into Rosalita's Cantina, a Tex Mex-style restaurant. Taking a seat at the bar, Farrah ordered a frozen margarita. Within seconds she'd downed the entire drink and had ordered another.

"Thirsty?" the guy next to her asked.

Farrah looked to her left and stared at him. He was a white guy who looked to be no older than thirty-three years old.

"You can say that," she replied, gulping down half of her second drink.

"Damn you really goin' through those. The next one's on me, a'ight?"

"Thanks," Farrah said, focusing in on the NBA finals pre-game show.

"Who you goin' for, the Mavericks or the Heat?" the guy asked.

"Neither," Farrah replied as tears built in her eyes.

During the season she and Khalil had rooted for the Bulls hard. Since they broke up she hadn't watched a basketball game, and to see one now only brought back happy memories of the time they used to share.

"I ain't tryin' to be all up in yo' business but are you cryin'?" The guy leaned forward to get a better view of her face.

Farrah hadn't even realized she'd begun to cry again. Running her fingers underneath her eyes she said, "No. My eyes are just sweatin'."

"Okay." The guy chuckled, handing her a napkin. "You sure you're all right?"

"Yes!" Farrah snatched the napkin from his hand.

"A'ight." The guy sat back in his seat.

A few minutes of silence passed then the guy sat up and said, "I'm Nick." He stuck his hand out for a shake. "And you are?"

"Not interested." Farrah rolled her eyes.

"Damn it's like that?" Nick chuckled.

"Listen." Farrah turned to the side and gave him her full attention. "You seem like a nice guy and all but I just came here to clear my mind and have a few drinks. So if you don't mind, I'd like to be left alone."

"Actually I do, 'cause you are way too fine to be sittin' here sulkin' over a man who probably ain't shit no way."

"And what makes you think I'm trippin' off of a man?"

"'Cause the sadness in your eyes could only be the result of a man."

Normally, Farrah didn't go for white guys. She'd dated one or two in the past but her dick of choice was chocolate or caramel. Nick on the other hand was an exception to the rule. He was drop-dead beautiful. His brown hair and comforting brown eyes instantly drew her in. The bitchiness she was servin' up was immediately put on reserve.

"Farrah." She smiled, extending her manicured hand.

"Huh?" Nick looked at her, confused.

"My name, it's Farrah."

"Oh." Nick laughed quietly. "Nice to meet you, Farrah." He took her hand in his and shook it.

Four margaritas, two Patrón shots, and nonstop laughter later, Farrah found herself inside Nick's red Mercedes G-Wagen ripping his clothes off. Kings of Leon's chart-topping hit "Sex on Fire" played loudly from the radio as she eagerly kissed his lips. Farrah knew she was acting totally out of character but for once she didn't care.

She wanted to know what it felt like to be wild, reckless, and free. She'd never see Nick again so why not live out one of her fantasies. Right there in the parking lot as the moon shone up above, Farrah rode his dick. Each thrust made her forget about her troubles and when she came she felt like a new woman.

"Damn I needed that," she panted, easing her way over to the passenger seat.

"Me too." Nick zipped up his jeans. "So . . . can I get your number?" he asked and smiled.

"You can give me yours." Farrah smiled back, handing him her phone.

"Ain't nobody gon' stalk you." Nick scrunched up his forehead.

"I know you not. That's why I'm taking your number."

"You better be glad you cute." Nick placed his number inside her phone, then handed it back to her.

"I'll call you." Farrah winked her eye as she got out, knowing she never would.

"Heffa! Where have you been?" London asked as soon as she walked through the door. "I have been callin' you for the past four hours. Oh my God, please don't tell me that muthafucka came over here trippin', 'cause this time I don't give a fuck what you say; I'ma fuck him up."

"We argued but that's not headlining news. Guess what I just did?" Farrah led London over to the couch and they both sat down.

"What?"

"I just had a one-night stand with this guy I just met at Rosalita's." Farrah smiled, pleased with herself.

"You lyin'? Get the fuck outta here."

"I swear." Farrah put her right hand up to God.

"Okay, yo' ass is gettin' a li'l bit off the chain now."

"I know." Farrah beamed.

"Don't get me wrong. I'm happy you're stickin' up for yourself and doing stuff you don't normally do but slow down, li'l mama. You can't just go around fuckin' random dudes. He could've had something."

"Huuuuuuuh spoil the moment, Debbie Downer."

"I'm just sayin'."

"I know you're right but it just felt so damn right." Farrah leaned back and gazed at the ceiling.

"I bet it did, Montana Fishburne," London joked.

"Ha ha ha funny." Farrah hit her with the middle finger.

"Did you at least get his name?"

"Yeah, it's Nick and guess what? He was white."

"'Bout time you got you some white meat. Ain't nothin' wrong wit' a li'l whole milk every now and then. It does a body good."

"You are such a freak. Is there a race you haven't slept wit' yet?"

London placed her hand under her chin and thought for a second. "Indian. I swear you can't find none of them muthafuckas nowhere."

The one thing Farrah loved more than anything in life was going to work. It was the greatest joy in her life. Every day she got to go to the Glam Studio and be among racks of designer clothes, shoes, jewelry, and makeup. There was never a day that went by that she didn't get to play dress-up.

That morning she and London, along with their assistant Camden, were going over looks for their clients who were attending the BET Awards. Now that their name was growing in the industry they were given the chance to style Eve, Tracee Ellis Ross, Nicki Minaj, and Teddy. After doing such a good job on the *Complex* magazine shoot, Farrah and London had to prove themselves even more. The pressure was on to kill it on the red carpet and Farrah was up for the challenge.

"I really like the Galliano T-shirt with the sequin harem pants and YSL pumps for Eve. What do you think?" Farrah held the pants up in front of her.

"I love it," Camden said, handing her a cup of coffee.

"If we do that look then I most definitely wanna do a soft face on her since the outfit is so edgy." London sat down and crossed her legs.

"I agree." Farrah nodded.

"Me too," Camden agreed. "I love the pale pink lip and cheek that you've created on your face chart." She looked down at the paper.

"Right, ain't it cute? Shit, I might do this face on me tonight when I go out." London stuck out her tongue.

"Where you going?" Farrah turned and looked at her.

"We're," London corrected her, "going over Teddy's house tonight."

"You say what now?" Farrah cocked her head to the side.

"He's having a card party-slash-barbeque tonight."

"What's that got to do with me?"

"Whatever, Farrah." London ignored her sarcasm. "You're going. Camden, if you wanna come you're more than welcome."

"Thanks, but me and my boyfriend are going out tonight."

"Uh excuse me." Farrah waved her hand back and forth in front of London's face. "I am not going with you tonight."

"Okay, Farrah, if you don't wanna go stay yo' li'l tired ass at home. Who cares?" London waved her off.

"Thank you." Farrah smiled.

"Anyway yo' phone is ringing." London handed her her phone.

Farrah gazed down at the screen and her smile grew even wider.

"Whaaaaaaat? Corey Mills know how to pick up the phone and call somebody," she teased.

"You know it ain't even nothin' like that. I just been hella busy that's all."

"I'm just fuckin' wit' you." Farrah walked across the room to get some more privacy. "How you been?"

"I'm makin' it. You?"

"Good. I'm actually going over a couple of looks for the BET Awards. London and I have a couple of people we're dressing."

"That's what's up. You doing yo' thang, ma."

"Thanks."

"As a matter of fact I might have you put something together for me and Jade. I'ma be opening my new tattoo shop in a few weeks. The press gon' be there and I'm having a step and repeat so we gotta look good."

"We would love to dress you and Jade for your shop's opening," Farrah said loudly so London could hear.

London's jaw dropped.

"I'ma holla at Jade about it and get back wit' you. But uh the reason why I was callin' is because my boy Teddy is having a li'l get-together at his crib tonight and I was gon' see if you wanna come."

"Actually London just told me about it. I'ma ride over there with her."

"Oh, really?" London spun around stunned. "You are really something. You know that? You are really something."

Farrah shot her the evil eye and mouthed, "shut up."

"Bet. I'll see you there then."

"Okay."

"Yep." Mills hung up.

"I swear you are the fakest bitch I know." London rocked back and forth like a ghetto girl. "When I asked you to go yo' yellow ass didn't want to but Mills ask you to go and yo' panties damn near fall off."

"Suck it." Farrah gave her the middle finger.

"If Teddy play his cards right, I just might."

Chapter Seven

There are certain feelings that I have for you. They've been bubblin' since the day that we were introduced.
—Carl Thomas feat. Brandy, "Somethin' Bout You"

By the time Farrah and London got to Teddy's place, the party was in full swing. The smell of smoky barbeque engulfed their noses as they walked through the door. The smell was so potent it made Farrah's stomach growl.

"Am I droolin'?" she whispered to London.

"No, but I think I am. There go Teddy." London looked across the room at him.

She could spot him all the way outside on the balcony turning over meat at the barbeque pit. His back was facing her. His shirt was off and she had a clear view of his toned, muscular back and all of the tattoos that adorned it.

"He is a cutie. A li'l on the young side but cute," Farrah said.

"That's the way I like 'em: young, dumb, and full of cum." London raised her hand for a high five.

"Uh, no." Farrah shook her head. "Pull yourself together so we can go say hi."

"Hey, Teddy," she spoke.

"What up, Farrah." He turned around.

"The food smells delicious." She gave him a hug.

"And so does your homegirl. Look at you." Teddy focused in on London. "You wearing them jeans, ma."

"I know." London turned around and twirled her butt in a circle.

"Is Mills here yet?" Farrah asked, looking around.

"He just walked in." Teddy pointed.

Farrah smiled brightly and stepped forward to go and say hi when she stopped dead in her tracks. Her smile promptly faded when she saw Mills walk in hand-in-hand with Jade. Farrah's heart continued to sink when Khalil and some chick walked in behind them. Khalil was with a completely different girl then she'd seen him with in the loop.

"You have got to be kidding me." London sucked her teeth.

"What the hell is he doing here?" Farrah's heart raced.

"Who?" Teddy questioned.

"Crackhead Khalil. You know him?" London screwed up her face.

"Yeah, that's my man. What y'all beefin' or something?"

"Khalil and Farrah just broke up and let's just say they didn't end on good terms."

"Oh well, I ain't know nothin' about that. You gon' be good?" Teddy asked Farrah, concerned.

"Yeah, I'm straight." Farrah swallowed. She didn't know whether she was more upset that Khalil was there, or that Mills had shown up with his girlfriend. She knew that they were strictly friends, but she couldn't help feeling someway about it.

"You wanna go?" London asked.

"Nah." Farrah shook her head. "I'm not gon' let him ruin my night. I've already let him ruin enough."

"Good girl. Just know if he start trippin' I'ma shank his ass."

"You're insane but I love you." Farrah wrapped her arm around London's shoulder and squeezed her tight. "Am I cute?" She let London go and stepped back so she could get a good view of her 'fit. She was wearing diamond-stud earrings, a floral-print blazer, Louis Vuitton necklace, gray slouchy T-shirt, vintage Levi's jean shorts, YSL tan ankle-strapped heels with a rose accent on the back, and a Hermès bag.

"Flawless, bitch. You killin 'em." London snapped her fingers as Mills spotted them.

"Ay, babe, let me go to speak to Farrah and her homegirl," Mills announced to Jade.

He knew that Farrah seeing Khalil with another girl would be difficult so he wanted to make sure she was okay. Instead of responding, Jade inhaled deep. Over the last six years she'd been around Farrah over a dozen times but she never really gave her the time of day. On top of the fact that Jade wasn't a girl's girl there was just something about Farrah she couldn't vibe with.

"You straight?" Mills whispered into Farrah's ear as he gave her a warm hug.

"Yeah. Did you know he was gon' be here?"

"Nah. You know I wouldn't even do you like that. We ran into him when we was gettin' on the elevator," he confirmed, stepping back as Jade took her place by his side.

"Hi, Jade." Farrah waved her hand weakly. Jade was always very standoffish with her so she never bothered to be too sociable with her.

"Farrah," Jade responded dryly.

"I don't know if you met my best friend, London, but, London, this is Mills's girlfriend, Jade. Jade, this is London," Farrah introduced them to one another.

"Hi," Jade spoke, looking the other way.

"Girl, please." London chuckled, unimpressed. "Let me go back over here wit' my boo before I have to get rowdy up in here. Mills." London gave him a head nod before returning to Teddy.

"We talked about it and Jade gon' pick out her own outfit for the shop opening but I want you to pick out some stuff for me," Mills said.

"Great, that's cool, Corey," Farrah replied with a smile. "You can come by the Glam Studio one day next week and try some stuff on."

Corey, Jade thought, screwing up her face.

"Bet but check it, I'll be back. Let me go introduce Jade to Teddy." Mills rubbed Farrah's arm.

"Okay." She forced a smile onto her face.

Finding herself alone once again, Farrah wondered how at the age of thirty she'd ended up a spinster. Her life was pathetic. She'd already run into Khalil with two different females on his arm after only three months of being apart. He stood only inches away from her and acted as if she didn't even exist. Then there was Mills. For years she'd secretly craved him but because of her past with Khalil he was off-limits.

Feeling like a complete loser, she found a seat on the couch and sat down. Gazing around, she took in the way Teddy had his place decorated. The wall behind her was painted a charcoal-gray shade. The color complemented the off-white couch and chair well. In the corner of the room was a life-sized aqua-blue ceramic vase with tons of bamboo sticks inside of it.

Farrah tried to focus on the ambiance but it was difficult when Khalil, his arm candy, Mills, and Jade held a conversation right in front of her face that consisted of them laughing hysterically.

Mills chuckled at Khalil's joke while never taking his eyes off of Farrah. He wanted nothing more than to go kick it to her and bring her a moment of happiness, but his main priority was Jade. Since he returned from New York they'd been doing well. Her attitude had gone from a level ten down to two, which was good.

They'd even been spending more time with each other. Mills chalked it up in his mind that what Farrah said was true. Their last few months of hell was just a rough patch. Now that things were back to normal Mills could rest comfortably knowing everything in his life was okay.

"What y'all gettin' into after y'all leave here?" Khalil asked, drinking a Modelo beer.

"I don't know. What you got planned?" Mills asked.

"We gon' hit up the strip club."

"I'm good, cuz." Mills shook his head.

"Why? I wanna go," Jade chimed in.

"You serious?" Mills asked, stunned.

"Yeah, it's like a club in there anyway."

"I know that. The question is how do you? When I tried to get you to go the strip club wit' me a year ago you acted like that was the worst thing I could'a ever done."

Caught up, Jade responded, "A couple of people I know told me that." She really knew because she and Rock had been there on several different occasions.

"Yeah," Mills replied, not fully believing her.

"Y'all rollin' or what?" Khalil asked.

"We'll see."

Annoyed by his response, Jade shook her head and rolled her eyes. Mills never wanted to do anything spontaneous anymore. With him it was always the same routine: go out to eat or see a movie then go back home and fuck.

"So did you speak to Farrah?" Mills questioned Khalil.

"Nah, what I'm gon' speak to her for? We ain't got shit to say to each other." He turned up his face.

"I just asked you a question, my dude. It ain't even that serious. I just thought you'd at least speak to the girl. Y'all was together for, what . . . four years."

"Fuck her." Khalil took a swig of his beer, upset. "I'd rather raw dog a beehive than speak to that bitch."

Mills sucked his teeth and tried to ease his rising temper. Khalil was his homeboy but he'd witnessed first-hand the way he dogged Farrah. She'd been an exceptional girlfriend to him, and instead of appreciating the good woman he was blessed with he took his blessing for granted.

"I gotta take a leak. I'll be back." Mills gave Jade a quick peck on the lips. He had to step away before he ended up saying something to Khalil he'd regret.

While Mills was off taking a piss Jade received a text message from Rock that read:

> From: Renee
> Can u get away?
> Received: Fri, June 10, 8:45

Just in case Mills ever decided to go through her phone, or if he saw a text come through her phone from Rock, she put his number in her phone under a girl's name. Ecstatic that he wanted to see her she replied:

To: Renee
Yeah but give me a min
Sent: Fri, June 10, 8:46

Jade placed her phone back inside her purse and imagined all the freaky things she and Rock were about to get into. Now that she'd heard from him, the whole devoted girlfriend act was done. Yeah, Rock had made it clear that what they shared was nothing but a sex thing, but in Jade's mind he had to care for her way more then he let on.

If he wasn't digging her then why would he constantly go out of his way to spend time with her? Besides that she couldn't stay away from him if she tried. She was trapped inside his web and couldn't get out. Every second she was away from him she missed him like crazy. Jade didn't know how she was going to get away to be with Rock that night. But she had to find a way because nothing mattered but getting to him.

"You hungry?" Mills asked, returning from the bathroom.

"A little," Jade responded.

"Ay, we about to head out," Khalil announced.

"Already?" Mills asked, surprised.

"Yeah, I just wanted to show my face." Khalil gave him pound.

"That's what's up. Y'all be safe."

"Yep. Hit my phone if y'all gon' come across the water," Khalil said over his shoulder.

"I will."

Farrah watched as Khalil and his girl left the party. She hated that his mere presence could affect her mood so negatively. She was so sick of being sad and hurt over him. He'd moved on so why hadn't she? Why couldn't she put their relationship out of her mind like he'd clearly done? Why couldn't she laugh and smile and be happy?

Why was it that their breakup was harder on her then it was him? Hell she'd walked away with no regrets so why was it that every morning she woke up she wished she hadn't? Her entire body felt like one big, gigantic tear. She wanted him to feel the same. But Khalil seemed happier than ever, which fucked her up mentally.

"Stop it." London plopped down next to her.

"Stop what?" Farrah blinked.

"Sittin' over here lookin' sad."

"Is it that obvious?"

"Yeah, and you need to stop. There are some tenders up in here who are dyin' to get wit' you but you too stuck on that deadbeat to notice." London glared at her.

"There's only one person here I wanna give my time to and he's taken," Farrah said, staring at Mills lovingly.

London followed Farrah's gaze and cocked her head to the side in disbelief. "And what's stoppin' you from gettin' on him? I know you ain't lettin' that trashbox get in yo' way. Girl, that bitch is a ho.com. I can look at her and tell she cheatin'."

"Whether she is or isn't ain't got nothin' to do wit' it. I wouldn't want nobody to do me like that so, no. I'ma keep my feelings to myself like I've been doin'," Farrah tried to tell herself.

"That's on you. In a minute we gon' play I Never, so get ready to get white girl wasted." London slapped her thigh and got up.

Once everyone had eaten, they all sat in Teddy's living room playing the drinking game I Never. Farrah was two shots into the game when it was her turn to go.

"I never . . . had a threesome," she said.

"Really, bitch?" London and five other people took a drink.

"Damn, shorty, you get down like that?" Teddy looked at her mischievously.

"Fall back, boo. It only happened once when I was in college."

"That's what they all say," Jade scoffed.

"Bitch, kill yo'self," London spat back.

"Uh," Teddy said, outdone. "Mills, it's your turn."

"All right," he said. "I never been locked up."

"Awwwwww!" the crowd roared.

"Nigga, that even right," Teddy said, taking a shot along with half of the room. "Baby, it's your turn." He patted London on her ass.

"Oooooooh, I got a good one." She danced in her seat. "In the last couple of weeks I never had a one-night stand wit' a white guy."

"Oh, yo' ass is tryin' to be funny." Farrah gave her the evil eye. "That ain't even how the game go but I'ma take a drink anyway." She took her shot.

For the second time that night Mills found himself getting heated. He shouldn't have cared what Farrah did sexually on her own time, but just knowing that she'd given it up to someone other than him pissed him off to the fullest extent. Jade was sitting next to him and didn't even notice the grimace plastered on his face. She was too busy checking her phone. Rock had sent her another message but this time it was a picture message.

Jade slyly turned to the side to open it and found the words, Still can't get away, with a picture of his hard dick underneath it. Turned on by the image Jade sat frozen stiff. She was so shaken that she hadn't even heard London calling her name.

"Trashbox!" London shouted, getting her attention.

"What?" Jade blinked, causing everyone to laugh.

"Oops I mean, Jade, it's your turn." London shot her a wicked smile.

"That was the last time, heffa," Jade snarled, coyly putting her phone in her pocket. "Okay." She pulled herself together. "I never . . . broke my arm."

Two people took a shot but to her surprise Mills didn't.

"Baby, why you ain't take a drink?"

"I'm done. I don't wanna play no more," he replied, clearly angry.

"Okaaaaay." Jade's eyes bucked.

"Yeah, that's enough," Teddy agreed. "It's gettin' late and I can't have y'all gettin' no DUIs on my account." He stood up.

"You ready?" Mills asked Jade.

"Yeah," she answered, wondering why he was upset.

"Y'all gettin' ready to go?" Farrah walked up to Mills.

"Yeah." He looked the other way. "Babe, go unlock the door for me. I'll be there in a minute." He held his keys out.

Jade took the keys from his hand and eyed him quizzically before walking off.

"I wasn't sure at first but I'm glad I came. I ended up having fun." Farrah smiled brightly.

"Good for you."

"Ewww. What's up wit' the stank attitude?" She scrunched up her forehead.

"So you goin' around fuckin' random white boys?" Mills barked.

Shocked by his question, Farrah stood silent for a second. "I mean it was nothin'," she finally uttered.

"Obviously."

"I'm confused. Why are you mad? We're just friends, right?" she questioned.

"Oh, fa'sho and that's all we gon' ever be since I see you on some ho shit," he snapped.

But once the venomous words crossed his lips he regretted it.

"Fuck you, Mills," Farrah snapped, stomping away.

"Farrah!" Mills called out only for her to ignore him.

Unbeknownst to him Jade had reentered the house and witnessed Farrah walking away mad and him calling her name.

"I couldn't get the door to open," she spoke up.

Mills faced her and took the keys from her hand.

"C'mon." He bypassed her.

On the way home Jade turned the radio down and said, "So what was up between you and ol' girl?"

"What you talkin' about?" Mills eyed the road carefully.

"Why she walk away from you upset?"

"I don't know."

"And why all of sudden you didn't want to play the game no more?" Jade questioned, not missing a beat.

"'Cause I got tired."

"You sure it ain't have nothin' to do wit' what her homegirl said?"

"Nah."

"You sure?" Jade pressed.

She wasn't really worried about Mills steppin' out on her wit' Farrah; okay, maybe a little. But, for the sake of starting an argument so she could have an excuse to get out of the house, she pretended like she was threatened by their friendship.

"I'm very sure," Mills assured her.

"Well, I'm not. You sure it ain't nothin' going on between y'all?"

"I told you it wasn't." Mills tried to sound convincing.

"Then why the fuck were you callin' her name like you were starring in a telenovela?"

"Are you really serious right now, or are you tryin' to start an argument?" Mills turned his head and looked at her.

"Don't switch this shit around on me, nigga!" Jade said, becoming angry for real. Maybe there was something to her line of questioning. "And, why the fuck she call you by your first name? What is that shit about?" She looked him up and down with disgust. "I don't even call you Corey."

"Uhhhhhhh, 'cause it's my name," Mills answered mockingly.

"Oh, you tryin' to be funny?" Jade arched her eyebrow.

"You need to calm the fuck down."

"I don't need to do shit!" Jade said, enraged.

"Who the fuck you yellin' at?" Mills turned and looked at her.

"You! Do you call yo'self likin' this chick? 'Cause if so let me know!"

"No. I like you but right now you makin' it real hard to."

"Mills, please! Save that slick shit for somebody who don't know you! Hold up! Now that I think about it, you didn't wanna play the game no more after what's-her-face made that comment about ol' girl having a one-night stand!"

"If that's what you wanna think," Mills said, pulling onto the parking lot of their building.

"You ain't left me no choice but to believe that, so you know what, since you like that bitch so much go spend the rest of the night wit' her!" She got out and slammed the door.

"Are you fuckin' kidding me?" Mills yelled out the window.

Jade didn't even bother to respond. Giving him her ass to kiss she hopped into her Benz and sped off.

Chapter Eight

**I'm the one you really want but you just
can't see it.
—Jill Scott feat. Eve, "Shame"**

For damn near a half hour Mills sat in the parking lot of his building waiting for Jade to pick up the phone, but she never did. The phone just rang and rang until her voice mail picked up. Mills was livid. He wasn't the type of dude to be all on a female's voice mail leaving messages. Recording his emotions for her to let her girlfriends possibly listen to later wasn't even an option.

He also wasn't the kind of man to be blowin' up his chick's phone all night no matter how much he loved her. There were just certain things you didn't do as a man and hounding a female like a li'l woman was one of them. If Jade was bold enough to disrespect him again then he would give her the space she obviously wanted and do him.

This shit wit' Jade showing her ass had been going on long enough. Mills was growing tired of asking her what the problem was and her saying she was good only to cop attitudes, not answer his calls, and be gone all the time wit' her so-called girlfriends. For months the notion that she might be cheating lingered in the back of his mind but Mills couldn't even stomach the thought.

For six years Jade had been his baby, his best friend. They'd been through it all. He'd given her nothing but the best of him and the best of what the world had to offer. Over the years Mills had plenty of opportunities to dick down other chicks, but the love he had for her overshadowed any nut that could potentially cost him his relationship.

He just prayed that she felt the same way, because if Mills ever found out differently there was no telling what he might do. Feeling his phone vibrate Mills gazed down at the screen hoping to see Jade's name, but instead Khalil's name came up.

"What up?"

"You still at Teddy's?" Khalil asked as a vision of Farrah's face crossed Mills's mind.

"Uh . . . naw. I'm back at the crib. Why? What's up?" he asked, trying to focus on the conversation.

"We just left Lola. I'm about to head across the water, man. You coming?"

"Nah, I'm good. I'ma kick back."

"A'ight. Li'l lame-ass dude. I'll get up wit' you later," Khalil teased.

"Yep." Mills hung up.

Given that Jade was on some bullshit and Mills didn't feel like being alone, he dialed Teddy's number.

"Hello?"

"Y'all still partying?" Mills asked him.

"It's a few people still here. What, you gon' swing back through?"

"I was thinkin' about it. Is Farrah still there?"

"Yeah. You wanna holla to her?"

"Nah, I'ma slide through though."

"A'ight." Teddy ended the call.

Bumpin' Trey Songz's "Me 4 U Infidelity 2," Mills made his way back to Teddy's. He was kind of happy Jade was actin' up 'cause now he'd get to spend some one-on-one time with Farrah without any unwanted eyes and ears around. But after their exchange she might not have been too pleased to see him. He'd let his emotions get the best of him and hurt her feelings in the process.

Now Mills had to perform damage control. Farrah's friendship meant way too much for him to see her in pain on the strength of him. The real

question was, how long would he be able to keep
up with the strictly friends facade before his true
feelings for her came pouring out? Each time he
came in contact with her his feelings grew more
and more. And with the way Jade was behaving,
it was only a matter of time before Mills said,
"fuck it," and put it on Farrah in the worst way.

At Teddy's house, Mills turned the knob and
walked in. "Sobriety" by Jesse Boykins III was
playing, creating a mellow atmosphere. The
lights were dimmed low but Mills could see
Teddy and London snuggled up on the couch. A
couple of other people were still there smoking
and drinking.

"Ay." Mills tapped Teddy on the shoulder.

Teddy gazed up at Mills and said, "Damn, you
wasn't bullshittin' was you?"

"I told I was coming back. Where Farrah at?"

"She on the balcony," London answered instead. "But let me tell you one thing. You come at
her sideways like that again, it's gon' be me and
you, you dig?"

"No worries. It won't happen again." He
laughed, heading toward the balcony.

"Am I laughin'? 'Cause I could'a swore I
wasn't." London looked at Teddy. "Oh, I see, he
must take me for a punk."

"Will you shut up and kiss me." Teddy turned her face toward him.

"You ain't said nothin' but a word, daddy." She passionately kissed him on the lips.

Mills stepped out onto the balcony and watched as Farrah sat gazing at the stars as rain poured from the midnight sky. Her shoes were off and she'd set her feet between the bars so drops of rain could fall on her toes. She seemed so at peace and content. Mills would have given anything to feel the same. Everything with Farrah was so easy. Despite all of the negativity in her life she still someway seemed to find a slice of joy.

"Farrah," he said softly.

"What?" she responded, not bothering to look his way.

"Can I talk to you for a minute?"

"Say what you got to say," she answered with an attitude.

"Can you turn around?"

Farrah let out a long sigh and slowly spun around. "You happy now?" she shot scornfully.

"I wanted to tell you I'm sorry for callin' you a ho." He laughed. "That was wrong and I don't feel that way about you at all."

"Frankly, I don't give a damn if you did," she lied; Mills's opinion of her really did matter.

"But evidently you do feel that way, or else you wouldn't have said it."

"I was just mad. I ain't mean that shit for real."

"How do you feel, Corey?" Farrah cocked her head to the side.

"On the real, Farrah, I don't know. My mind is so fucked up right now."

Farrah thought about pressing the situation but saw no point. If Mills wanted her he'd make it known. And since the kiss he'd made it a known fact that she and he were nothing but homeboy and homegirl.

"Why you decide to come back?" Farrah quizzed.

"'Cause I wanted to talk to you."

"Jade ain't mad?"

"Does . . . it . . . matter?"

Farrah giggled because it didn't.

"How long you plan on stayin' here?" he asked.

"For a li'l while longer. Why? You gon' have a drink with me?" Farrah smiled.

"You must've read my mind."

For the next few hours Mills, Farrah, Teddy, London, and the last few partygoers played *Wii Sports,* drank, and enjoyed each other's company. It was almost three when everyone left. Farrah was tipsy and tired as hell but didn't want to leave because she was taking pleasure in kickin' it wit' Mills.

"Ahhhhhhh," she yawned, stretching her arms.

"You sleepy?" Mills inquired, lying on the couch.

"A little bit."

"Well, friend, I'm spending the night here." London got up. "So what you gon' do? You stayin' here or going home?"

"Why would I stay here wit' you and Teddy? I'm going home."

"Shit, London told me you wanted to have a threesome wit' us," Teddy joked.

"Boy, don't play." London slapped him on the arm.

"Anyway." Farrah laughed.

"All jokes aside if y'all wanna stay y'all more than welcome. If not lock the door on your way out." Teddy picked London up and carried her up the stairs.

"Let me get outta here while I'm still coherent enough to drive." Farrah went to stand up but Mills pulled her back down.

"Lie here wit' me for a minute."

Farrah gladly did as she was told and lay in a spooning position with him. So they could lie comfortably Mills wrapped her up in his arms. The top of her head rested under his chin. Their bodies fit together perfectly. Neither felt guilty or uncomfortable about their closeness. Everything about the moment seemed blessed and predestined.

Snuggled back to chest they closed their eyes and allowed a peaceful dream state to take place. Then the sun came into full bloom and they were awakened by the sound of London's voice calling Farrah's name.

"Huh," she groaned.

"Time to get up, sleepyhead. We gotta bounce." London shook her thigh.

"Why?" Farrah whined, not wanting to move.

"'Cause we have clients. Now get up." London pulled her up by the arm.

"Okay," Farrah pouted, sitting up straight.

"Damn what time is it?" Mills asked, rubbing his eyes.

"Eight o'clock." Teddy came down the steps in only his boxers and a pair of hoopin' shorts.

"Let me take my ass home." Mills got off the couch. Mills retrieved his cell phone from his pocket and saw that Jade had called him twice.

"What you gettin' into later on?" He looked down into Farrah's eyes.

"The bed," she joked, yawning.

"I feel you on that one. But, uh, last night was cool." Mills placed his hands inside his pockets.

"It was." Farrah blushed.

"Okay, y'all can cake it up later. We gotta go," London said.

"Let me go before I have to punch this chick in the throat."

"A'ight, I'll walk y'all out." Mills unlocked the door.

The whole ride home Mills anticipated walking through the door and finding Jade on a warpath ready to kill. Since they'd been together he'd never once not come home. But how much more could a man take when his woman was shooting bullets into his heart at close range? Placing his key into the door he prepared himself to be cussed out royally. Mills walked into the house and went directly to his and Jade's bedroom and found her lying in bed watching television.

"Hi," she spoke sweetly.

"What's up?" he said, caught off guard by how calm she was. "What time you get in last night?" he asked.

"Around three something," Jade responded.

"You have fun?" Mills took off his jacket.

"Yep, you?" Jade turned the channel.

"I guess you can say that." Mills kicked off his shoes.

Jade kept her focus on the television and chuckled.

"Well, I'm gettin' ready to get in the shower."

"Okay. You want something to eat?" She smiled, fuckin' wit' him.

"Nah, I'm good." He eyed her, perplexed.

Thoroughly confused, Mills went into the master bathroom and closed the door behind him. Jade hadn't reacted at all the way he thought she would. He'd stayed out all night and she acted as if nothing ever happened. Most women would've flipped out, but not Jade. Mills didn't know what part of the game this was, but whatever part it was he didn't like it one bit.

While Mills took a shower Jade lay in bed channel surfing. Sure, she wanted to go off about him not coming home, but in Jade's mind she wouldn't clown with him. No, she would bite her tongue, because when she returned the favor and stayed out all night he wouldn't be able to say a thing.

Chapter Nine

He got that thickness, the kind that makes you get up and do biscuits wit' breakfast, so gone.
—Jill Scott, "So Gone"

"'Cause we like to party! Ay, ay, ay, ay!" Jade and her best friend, Deion, sang while pulling up to Mimi's Nail Salon. It wasn't a posh nail shop but the nail techs were some of the best St. Louis had to offer, and they always stayed on top of the latest nail trends.

"Girl, that's my shit!" Deion said, grabbing her Louis Vuitton bag.

"Mine too. I love the part when Bey be like 'I told my girls you can get it,'" Jade sang, getting out of the car.

"Yeah, she most definitely did her thing wit' that song," Deion agreed.

"I will be bumpin' it for the rest of the night. And when we get to the party I'ma tell the DJ to play it, too," Jade said, pulling the nail salon's door open.

"What time you gon' start gettin' ready?" Deion followed in behind her.

"I guess about four-thirty." Jade glanced over the nail polish rack for a color.

"We have to be there no later than six-thirty to take pictures for the paps and so Mills can talk to the press."

"I can't wait. The dress I bought is too cute." Deion popped her lips. "What color you gon' get yo' nails?"

"Pink I think, you?" Jade looked at her.

"I'ma get mine black." Deion picked up the shade.

"That'll be cute."

"I know." Deion smirked.

"What you need done today?" one of the nail techs asked the ladies.

"Eyebrow arch, fill in, and a pedicure," Jade answered.

"Me too," Deion agreed.

"Come sit down." The nail tech pointed to two empty pedicure chairs.

"So what's been going on wit' you and Mills?" Deion took a seat as Jade's phone rang.

"Hold up; this Jahquita." Jade rolled her eyes.

Jahquita was Deion and Jade's girlfriend from the old neighborhood, who wasn't as stylish or pretty as they were. Jahquita was a size twenty-two but you couldn't tell her she wasn't the shit. Homegirl had humongous tits, a beer belly, wide hips, and an ass that would put Buffie the Body to shame but that didn't stop her from dressing like a video vixen.

"Hello?" Jade answered, taking off her Chanel sandals.

"Hey, girl. What you doing?" Jahquita smacked on a piece of gum.

"Me and Deion at the nail shop gettin' our nails done."

"Y'all ballin'." Jahquita continued to smack. "I wish I could get my nails done, 'cause I sholl need it and my feet look a mess.org. They all crusty and shit but Section 8 done went up on my rent again."

"For real? How much you gotta pay now?" Jade pretended to care, putting her feet in the hot water.

"Fifty-eight dollars. Can you believe that? I am pissed off."

"I would be too, girl." Jade stifled a laugh. "But anyway you ready to party, girl?"

"Hell, yeah!" Jahquita popped her lips.

"Then put on yo' funeral clothes 'cause we about to kill these muthafuckas tonight." Jade snapped her fingers.

"You ain't said nothin' but a word. My outfit is the shit. You know Dots be e-mailing me those percent-off coupons so me and the kids went yesterday and picked me out a li'l somethin' somethin'," Jahquita bragged.

"Girl, how all y'all fit into that li'l bitty-ass car?" Jahquita drove a Kia Sephia.

"We make it do what it do, baby! Jahquita Jr. sat up in the front wit' me and January, Al' Walid, Javontay, Alquita, and Versacharee sat in the back wit' the twins on they lap."

"Wow," Jade said, astonished. "What you end up gettin'?"

"I got this real cute yellow tube top, zebra-print leggings, and these hot pink strappy heels," Jahquita said excited.

"That sound cute. Well, good for you, girl. Look let me get off this phone. They starting on my nails," Jade lied.

"Okay, I'll call you later." Jahquita ended the call.

"You are so fake." Deion laughed.

"Ain't I?" Jade laughed too. "Girl, she gettin' ready to look a hot mess.com."

"Why you invite her?" Deion questioned.

"How could I not? Everybody knows about the grand opening. I had to invite her."

"Whatever, that's on you. That's your friend." Deion pointed her index finger in Jade's direction.

"She yo' friend too." Jade pointed out.

"I ain't claiming that rachetness." Deion chuckled. "Anyway back to what I was sayin'. What's going on wit' you and Mills?"

"Girl, I don't know." Jade placed her hand on her forehead. "We got into it real bad a couple of weeks ago. I mean I started the fight 'cause I was tryin' to go see Rock—"

"Oh my God," Deion groaned.

"Shut up, listen. It's this chick named Farrah—"

"Oh, I remember her; she's cute," Deion cut her off.

"She look a'ight." Jade curled her upper lip. "Now listen. I think it might be something going on between the two of them."

"Get the fuck outta here." Deion gasped. "Are you serious?"

"I mean I don't have any proof or anything but she calls him by his first name and they be having these side conversations and shit. I don't know. I'ma have to keep an eye on them." Jade gazed absently at the bubbles surrounding her feet.

"Jade"—Deion cocked her head to the side—"are you insane, or just plain crazy?"

"What?" Jade shrugged her shoulders.

"How you gon' keep an eye on anybody when you out here suckin' another man's dick on a regular?"

"Girl and I love it. Rock's dick is like Hogwarts. It holds all the magic inside," Jade shimmied in her seat.

"Yeah, I'm not gon' even respond. Anyway." Deion flicked her wrist. "How you gon' call yo'self keepin' an eye on Mills when you don't even show that man the time of day?"

"I know . . . I love Mills, I do, but there is just something about Rock." Jade closed her eyes and smiled.

"What?" Deion arched her eyebrow. "'Cause I don't see it."

"It's unexplainable. But you know what I think it is"—Jade pointed her finger—"he reminds me of how Mills used to be. We used to be on some ol' wild shit together. Now it's just like, been there done that."

"Well, heffa, if you want the romance back in your relationship how about tellin' Mills how you feel, instead of bonin' another nigga, jackass," Deion spat.

"You're right but—"

"It ain't no but, nigga," Deion checked her.

"Yeah, it is 'cause I want both of them."

"Okay." Deion nodded her head. "Let Mills find out what you been doing. He . . . gon' . . . beat . . . yo' . . . muthafuckin' . . . ass."

"Girl, Mills ain't gon' do shit. And what you trippin' off of it so hard for? You act like you wanna fuck him." Jade arched her eyebrow.

"Let me put you in yo' place real quick," Deion sat up straight. "I don't want yo' man 'cause I got one. But if I did want him, I would have 'em. I just know what's right and what's wrong. You don't do people like that. Karma is a bitch, honey, and when this shit come back on you, you better be ready."

"Anyway." Jade rolled her eyes to the ceiling. "Mills too busy ridin' bikes and openin' up tattoo shops to notice anything I do. I'm good."

"So you really think Mills don't know you out here cheatin'? Y'all been together six years and you ain't never acted like this."

"Like what?" Jade grinned.

"You think this shit is funny." Deion eyed her, surprised. "Bitch, you forever got an attitude for no damn reason. You always gone. Shit, from what you told me you never wanna have sex wit' him no more."

"Gurrrrrrrrrl, this might be TMI but awhile back me and Rock fucked so much that when Mills wanted some pussy I had to act like I wanted it in my ass just so he wouldn't know the difference." Jade giggled.

"You damn right. That was too much information," Deion said, disgusted as the nail tech scrubbed her feet.

"Whatever." Jade laughed. "I miss my baby too."

"Where he at?"

"In L.A. He'll be here next week to see me though." Jade poked out her bottom lip. "But that's cool. That way I can be there for Mills tonight and kick it wit' Rock all next week."

"And how do you spell whore?" Deion joked. "J-a-d-e." She laughed as Rock's ringtone started to play.

"Aww, here go my pooh-pooh now." Jade grinned, pressing answer. "Hi, pumpkin."

"What you doing?" Rock said into the phone.

"At the nail shop wit' Deion."

"Ay, I need you to do me a favor."

"Anything." Jade cherished the sound of his voice.

"I'm coming in town today. My flight lands at seven o'clock so can you pick me up from the airport?"

"Uhhhhh." Jade's eyes bucked. She hadn't expected this monkey wrench to be thrown into the mix. She figured she'd be able to play the supportive girlfriend all weekend, then get back to doing her in the week ahead. That way both men in her life would be satisfied. Now she had to make a decision and fast. It was either be there for her man who'd held her down from the beginning, or be there for the man she was addicted to. Someone was going to get played but, oh well. Jade would deal with the consequences later. "I thought you were coming out here next week."

"I got a break in my schedule so I decided to come early. What, you don't want me to come?"

"Nah, it's cool. Just call my phone when you land, babe," she assured him.

"Good lookin' out. You gon' give me some tonight?" Rock asked, dying to see her.

"You ain't know."

"Bet. Well, I'll see you at seven."

"Okay."

"Ay, before I let you go, I got a surprise for you when I get there," Rock teased.

"What is it?" Jade said, excited.

"It wouldn't be a surprise if I told you now would it?"

"No."

"A'ight then, Blondie, seven o'clock."

"Bye." She ended the call.

"Mmm mmm." Deion shook her head from side to side.

"What?" Jade stared at her, annoyed.

"Don't what me. Yo' ass gon' be the one on a stretcher not me. You are really showing out but that's on you. Handle yo' scandal."

"I can't just leave him at the airport. Plus he got a gift for me." Jade smiled from ear to ear.

"Why not?" Deion looked at her as if she were crazy. "That nigga got paper. He can catch a fuckin' cab. Hell, tell his ass to rent a camel or a mule something. Like, Jade, you really need to pull it together. You cannot miss Mills's grand opening."

"Why? It's not like I haven't been to the last four. Missing one ain't gon' hurt nothing. Besides he'll understand."

"How you figure that?"

"Watch." Jade dialed Mills's cell.

"What up?" he answered.

"Hey, babe, listen. I'ma be late tonight."

"Why?"

"'Cause I gotta take Deion to the emergency room," Jade lied.

"Are you fuckin' kiddin' me?" Deion whispered.

"Shut up," Jade mouthed.

"What's wrong wit' her?" Mills asked, concerned.

"She think she got a real bad bladder infection or something."

"Damn. I hope she'll be a'ight."

"She will be. She just gotta get some medication that's all."

"How long you think you gon' be?" Mills questioned.

"You know how the emergency room is. It depends, maybe three or four hours. I'ma try my best to wrap this up as quick as I can and I'll be there." Jade tried to sound convincing.

"A'ight, call me and let me know what they say when you get there," Mills said, disappointed that she'd miss half the party.

"I will. I love you." Jade blew a kiss into the phone.

"Love you too." Mills hung up.

"Bitch, are you and Satan BFFs? Do you got that nigga on speed dial? How in the hell you gon' burn bread on me like that?" Deion went off. "Now if I get a bladder infection for real I'ma slap the shit outta you. Then I'm gon' come back and slap the shit outta you again. Oh, and let me guess, since I got a so-called bladder infection"— Deion made air quotes with her hands—"and you wanna be a ho, I gotta miss the party?"

"I'm sorry, friend. I had no choice."

"Stop makin' excuses, bitch. You did have a choice. You just chose the wrong one."

"I promise I'll make it up to you." Jade patted her hand.

"You damn right you gon' make it up to me. I want those gold spiked Christian Louboutin booties in a size seven please."

"I got you." Jade sat back, pleased with herself.

"And you gon' pay for my nails and feet to be done," Deion said firmly.

Chapter Ten

**I'm sittin' here tryin' to keep my
composure knowing inside I'm broken
and tore up.
—Diddy-Dirty Money, "Yesterday"**

The grand-opening party for Mills's tattoo
shop was in full swing. DJ Needles was spin-
nin' all of the hottest hits and waiters strolled
the room passing around hors d'oeuvres. As a
thank you to his loyal customers Mills gave one
free tattoo to each guest in attendance. Farrah
wanted to get a small heart on her wrist but the
dance floor kept calling her name.

She, London, and Camden grooved to the beat
of Waka Flocka's strip club anthem "Round of
Applause" but she couldn't take her eyes off of
Mills. The same face he wore in New York was
back in full force. All night he faked being happy
when really, if you looked closely, you could see
he was dying on the inside. Instead of enjoying
his party throughout the night all he did was stay
on his phone.

Farrah knew his displeasure was due to Jade's absence. But Farrah wasn't going to let Jade ruin his night. She was determined to put a genuine smile on his face and make him see how blessed he was despite Jade not being there.

"I'll be right back," she told London and Camden before sashaying away.

"You are way too fine to be standing here lookin' like that."

"Lookin' like what?" Mills placed his phone inside his back pocket.

"Sad that's what. This is your party. You should be enjoying it. Not over here lookin' like you about to fuck everything in here up."

"It's just a lot going on." He rubbed his forehead.

"Unless somebody's dead or in the hospital, nothing is more important than this moment." Farrah rubbed his forearm.

Mills looked off to the side and massaged his jaw. Jade was back to her old tricks. It just sucked that she would decide to act like a bitch on one of the biggest nights of his life. She should've been there supporting him, but instead she was out doing God knows what and with whom. But, fuck that. Farrah was right. Mills wasn't going to let her inconsiderate behavior destroy everything he'd worked so hard for. The people who were there were all that mattered.

"C'mon let's get a drink." He placed his hand on the small of Farrah's back and led her over to the bar.

Mills was determined to get his mind off Jade no matter what. It wasn't like he could deal with the situation right then anyway. Mills was done. He wasn't going to continue to play himself by blowin' up Jade's phone all night and stressin' over her. It was time for him to do him.

With a few glasses of Nuvo and Grey Goose in his system Mills began to find his groove. He even found himself on the dance floor two-steppin' with Farrah to Drake's song "She Will" featuring T.I. Buzzed, he held her by the waist and repeated T.I.'s opening monologue, "I know you don't do this often but . . . I'm the exception. Do it for me, huh. Pop that pussy for a real nigga, ma."

Farrah simply smiled devilishly, turned around, and did exactly what she was told. Mills watched closely as her ass bounced to the beat. Suddenly, within a blink of an eye, any stress that he felt melted away and he found himself having a good time. He loved that about Farrah; whenever he was in a funk she always found a way to make him feel better. Fuck it, there was no more denying it. Farrah was the truth.

"Ay, I'm going to get another a drink. You want something?" he asked her.

"Nah, I'm good." She danced.

"I'll be right back." He looked her up and down lustfully before walking off.

Mills wasn't even gone a minute before one of the dudes at the party got on Farrah. With a fresh drink in his hand Mills headed back over to the dance floor when he saw a guy and Farrah dancing. The blood in his veins immediately started to boil. Mills clenched his jaw tight and placed his free hand inside his pocket. It never failed. He couldn't win for losing. Just when he was starting to have a good time Farrah had to go and put him in an even worse mood.

Wondering what was taking Mills so long to return, Farrah kindly patted the guy on the chest and sauntered off the dance floor. It didn't take her too long to find him. He was by his favorite place: the bar.

"I thought you was coming back," she said breathlessly.

"I was but you started dancing wit' ol' boy so I ain't wanna interrupt."

"You mad?" Farrah grinned. "I know you're not jealous," she joked.

"Of what, that nigga?" Mills mocked. "C'mon you know me better than that. I'm too fly to be jealous. Besides we ain't together. You ain't my girl."

For some reason Mills's words hurt Farrah and she found herself unable to breath. "You know what? You're right," she spat, stepping back.

"Chill out." Mills tried to grab her hand.

"No, you're right. I'm not your girl. I'm the chick who's here supporting yo' ass while yo' bitch is out fuckin' and suckin' somebody else. So before you cop an attitude wit' me you need to direct that shit toward the bitch you claim is your girl!" Farrah shouted before storming off.

Dressed in the clothes from the day before, Jade happily walked into her and Mills's bedroom a little after 8:00 a.m. Little did she know, Mills had been waiting patiently for her arrival since he'd gotten home the night before. He sat in a chair next to the window with an ounce of weed and bottle of Hennessy by his side.

Through the night he tried his hardest to kill the brain cells in his head, but like poison they kept eating away at him. He wished the tears inside of him would quit clouding his heart but it was inevitable. This was what misery felt like.

"Damn!" Jade held her chest, surprised. She naturally assumed Mills would be asleep. "What you doing up so early?" She placed her purse down.

"Where the fuck you been?" Mills said as calmly as he could.

"At Deion's house. After we left the hospital I ended up spending the night over there." She kicked off her heels.

"Lie number one." Mills balled his fist.

"What?" Jade eyed him sideways.

"I'ma ask you again and this time don't lie. Where you been?" Mills shot her a look that could kill.

Jade had no idea that before coming home Mills had driven past Deion's house and Jade's car was nowhere to be found.

"What are you talkin' about? I told you. I was at Deion's."

"I swear to God if you lie to me again I'ma knock yo' fuckin' head off." Mills's nostrils flared as he stood up. "Where the fuck you been?" he yelled, causing Jade to jump.

"Whoa-whoa-whoa, yoooooooou need to calm down. Hold your horses, homeboy." Jade held her hands up. "I already told you where I was so if you don't believe me that's all on you."

"It's on me?" Mills screwed up his face.

"Yeah," she scoffed, trying to walk toward the bathroom, but before she could take two steps forward Mills grabbed both of her arms.

"Are you fuckin' crazy?" Jade tried to break loose but couldn't.

"Shut the fuck up." Mills pushed her down onto the bed.

"I'm not playin' wit' you, Mills! Let me go!" Jade shouted, hoping to intimidate him.

"So you gon' sit here and lie to me like I'm some sucka-ass nigga! You wasn't at no fuckin' Deion's house! You was wit' that nigga!" He shook her.

Jade's heart stopped. *Oh my God, he knows.*

"What are you talkin' about?" She tried playing dumb. "I ain't fuckin' wit' nobody else!"

"I rode past Deion's house! Yo' ass wasn't there!" He gripped her neck.

"I was! I was I parked in the garage!" Jade yelled, barely able to breathe.

"I could fuckin' kill you, you know that?" Mills pressed his thumbs into her neck.

"Mills, I can't breathe." Jade slapped his arms profusely.

Realizing he was letting his emotions get the best of him, Mills quickly let her go.

"You have lost yo' fuckin' mind!" Jade held her neck and took several deep breaths. "You could've killed me! You fuckin' psycho! You fuckin' asshole! You're fuckin' insane!"

"Can't you see you killin' me?" Mills pounded his fist against his chest.

"You don't fuckin' get it." Jade shook her head.

"Get what?"

"I'm not happy!" Jade yelled, balling her fist.

"'Cause you cheatin'!"

"Ain't nobody cheatin' on you." Jade looked over to the side instead of in Mills's eyes.

"At least look me in the eye if you gon' lie."

Never the one to back down from a challenge, Jade stood up and got in Mills's face. Staring him directly in the eye, she said without blinking, "I'm not cheating on you."

Mills wanted to believe her, but everything about the moment, the unsure look in her eyes and the trembling of her lips, was foul.

"How long you been fuckin' him?" he asked calmly.

"Wow." Jade chuckled, shaking her head. "You are crazy and I sooo don't have time for this." She turned and walked toward their walk-in closet.

"You not gon' even say 'my bad' for missing the opening or nothin'? You just gon' pretend like everything you doing is good?" Mills felt his heart shrink with every word.

"Of course I feel bad that I missed the opening but my friend was sick. What was I supposed to do, just leave her?" Jade stripped down out of her clothes.

"So you still stickin' wit' that lie, no matter what?" Mills asked, feeling like he was dying on the inside.

All he wanted was the truth. Jade was feeding him nothing but lies and they both knew it. Jade was dead set on destroying everything they'd built over the last six years all because she was unwilling to tell the truth. Who knew, maybe if she confessed to her deceit Mills could find it in his heart to forgive her and try again. But then again maybe he couldn't forgive and move forward.

For six years they'd been doing nothing but coasting along and pretending like their relationship was perfect. When in all actually they were only with each other because of the time they'd invested in one another. Jade was all Mills knew and vice versa. He loved her with all of his heart but lately he'd begun to think, was loving her enough to keep him content?

"Think what you wanna think." Jade snatched an outfit down from a hanger. "It's obvious that you don't trust me so why are we together?"

"You're right. Why am I wit' you?" Mills massaged his jaw.

"Answer the question. Why are you wit' me? I trust you. I don't think that you're out there cheatin' on me—"

"'Cause I don't give you a reason to think that!" Mills cut her off.

"So I'm just a lyin', cheatin'-ass whore I guess." Jade shrugged her shoulders.

"You said it, I didn't."

"It's all good, Mills. Fuck you!" Jade pointed her finger toward him. "If you don't believe me then that's all on you! I know what it is so who gives a fuck about what you think!" She headed toward the bathroom to shower and dress.

"You care about what that other nigga think, don't you?" Mills shot.

"Whatever, Mills." Jade slammed the door shut behind her.

She wasn't about to let him ruin her day. She and Rock had just spent a romantic day and night together. After picking him up from the airport she dropped Deion off and took him to the Crowne Plaza hotel downtown to check in. Once all of that was taken care of she gave him the keys to her Jeep, which Mills had bought, so he could drive them to Frontenac Plaza.

Like Jade, Rock loved the finer things in life. Rock was very flashy and loved to show off. He had no problem droppin' stacks of dough on himself and others around him. After a few hours of nonstop shopping, he'd bought Jade five pairs of designer heels and ten designer outfits. Jade was over the moon. With all of her new merchandise she'd built up quite an appetite so they went to Ruth's Chris and had steak for lunch.

The rest of the day consisted of them making love in every position imaginable until neither could move. Jade enjoyed every waking second of being with Rock and didn't want to leave, but figured she'd deal with her and Mills's drama, then head back to the hotel.

Fresh and clean, Jade applied her makeup and slipped on her clothes. She couldn't move fast enough. Every second that she spent apart from Rock felt like an eternity. Dressed and ready to go she opened the door and found Mills sitting on the edge of the bed, waiting for her.

Oh my God, she thought picking out a pair of high heels. *He's still here?*

"Where you going?" Mills questioned.

"Out." Jade stacked her H&M friendship bracelets on her wrist.

"Word? So that's how we doing it now?" Mills probed.

He was trying his hardest not to explode on her again, but Jade was making it hard. She didn't give a damn about his feelings or the fact that he was hurting inside. He expected her to be remorseful but she wasn't. When he looked at her he saw nothing but a blank canvas. The last thing Mills wanted to do was play himself when it came to her, but after being with her so long he thought their relationship deserved a fighting chance before he threw in the towel and said "fuck it" too.

"Look, I'm not about to fight wit' you. I'm having a good day and you're not about to ruin it. If you think I'm cheatin' on you then break up with me." Jade stepped into her heels and stared him square in the eyes.

She was so high off her rendezvous with Rock that at that moment she didn't care if she and Mills stayed together.

"That's really how you feel?" Mills's heart shattered into pieces.

"Yes, 'cause I'm sick of you accusing me of a bunch of shit that ain't true so maybe we need to think about whether we need to be together."

"I agree." Mills nodded his head.

"Well, there you have it. I guess I'll see you later then." Jade put on her shades and headed out the door.

Mills sat still on the edge of the bed and waited for the sound of the door closing to hit him. Once it did he felt empty, like Jade had taken all of him with her. His heart wanted desperately to believe her when she said she was innocent of his accusations, but his mind knew better. He knew the game all too well and Mills knew he was being played. The question was, was he gonna stick around and be a pawn in Jade's chess game, or take his rightful place as king and do things his own way?

Chapter Eleven

**And I ain't even think 'bout the next chick
that he mess wit' . . . so reckless.**
—Jill Scott, "So Gone"

"I thought you weren't coming back until later," Rock said as Jade crossed the threshold to his hotel room.

"That was the plan until he pissed me off." Jade threw her YSL clutch down onto the bed. She normally didn't discuss Mills with Rock but today she needed to vent.

"What happened?" Rock locked the door.

"When I got back to my place he was there and we got into it 'cause I didn't come home last night. I mean I knew he was gon' be mad but I didn't expect him to put his hands on me."

"He hit you?" Rock asked, stunned. Swiftly he took her into his embrace.

"I don't even wanna talk about it." Jade choked up. She knew she should've made it clear that Mills didn't strike her, but the concerned expression on Rock's face was priceless and the way he held her in his arms felt too good to resist.

"Yo, you don't need to be puttin' up wit' that. Shouldn't no man be puttin' his hands on no woman. Has he ever done this before?" Rock held her at arm's length and stared into her eyes.

"Yeah," Jade lied. "Once before. It's like I don't even know him anymore. We don't spend time with each other. Every time I turn around he's out of town, probably wit' some chick. Hell, the last time you were here he jumped up and went to New York without me." Jade lied once more, loving the sympathy she was receiving from Rock.

"Why you still wit' him?"

"I mean . . . I do still care about him. We've been together six years. Besides what I'ma do just up and leave? Who knows how he might react." She began to cry.

"Stop that." Rock wiped her face. "You too pretty to be letting some nigga make you cry."

"I just hate that I let him make me feel this way. Especially after how good of a time we had yesterday."

"Yeah, yesterday was pretty fly." Rock smiled.

"It was." Jade laughed.

"That's what I like to see. Show me that pretty smile." Rock hugged her. "Fuck all that bullshit you dealin' wit' at home. You my baby and I ain't gon' let nobody hurt you."

Jade stood frozen in time. Everything from the time to her stopped. If she could've kissed God on the cheek she would've. She'd waited forever to hear those words come out of Rock's mouth. Sure, she hadn't been 100 percent honest with him about her and Mills's relationship. She'd made him out to be a monster, but Jade was willing to do anything—lie, embellish, or simply make up shit—to make Rock hers.

She knew he didn't want a woman, but she was determined to change his mind. She'd risked too much at this point to turn back now. She was head over heels in love with Rock. He was a great man and a dedicated father and she wanted nothing more than to be his girl.

"So, I'm your baby, huh," she finally whispered.

"Yeah, as a matter of fact come on." Rock stood up. "I got an idea. Let's go get matching tattoos."

"You for real?" Jade's face lit up.

"Yeah, now let's go before I change my mind."

With a few drinks in his system Mills chirped the alarm on his car and walked toward Farrah's door. Since their blowout at his party she'd been on his mind. He'd been terribly rude to her at the party and he owed her a huge apology. He only prayed that she'd accept it, because honestly he knew this time he'd taken things too far.

Inside of the house Farrah patted her face dry after washing her makeup off. Cee Lo Green's album *The Lady Killer* played in the background. It had been a long day and she wanted nothing more than to climb into bed and fall fast asleep, but just as she was putting on her nightly face cream the doorbell rang.

"Huhhhhhh," she groaned, rolling her eyes.

She just knew that it was London at the door because she was always leaving or losing her keys. Irritated, Farrah stomped down the stairs and unlocked the door without looking to see who it was.

"Bitch . . . my name is not Benson," she huffed, pulling the door open.

"Damn, I knew you was mad but why I gotta be a bitch?' Mills shot mockingly, leaning up against the door frame.

"What are you doing here?" Farrah asked, shocked to see him standing there.

"I came to see what was up wit' you? What? You want me to come back?" He stood up straight, prepared to leave.

"Nah, you good." Farrah slightly rolled her eyes and stepped to the side to let him in.

Sensing her attitude, Mills hesitantly walked inside and stood by the door. Farrah tried not to look at him but found it hard not to. Mills was rockin' the hell out of a pair of black Wayfarer shades, an all-black Tisa hoodie, black fitted jeans, and Jordan 4s. Farrah absolutely detested the hold his presence had over her. Just the sight of him made her body melt. Mills was fine beyond words but his attitude was for the birds.

Mills stood beside the door with his back up against the wall. Thankfully he had on shades because he couldn't keep his eyes off of her. Farrah was bad. All she wore was a white racer-back tank top and a pair of Juicy Couture cotton booty shorts that barely covered her ass cheeks. The simplistic outfit highlighted every area of her body that was priceless.

"So what's up?" Farrah folded her arms across her chest to cover up the fact that she wore no bra.

"What you been on today?"

"I went to work, to the laundromat, got my nails done, and went to the grocery store," she answered, making sure not to give him any eye contact. "Why?" she asked with an attitude.

"What you get from the grocery store?" Mills tried to prolong their small talk.

"Really, Mills?" Farrah cocked her head to the side. "What is it, 'cause I'm tired and I'm gettin' ready to go to bed. I ain't got time for a bunch of games."

"I just came by to say I'm sorry for last night. I wasn't tryin' to hurt your feelings—"

"Well, you did," Farrah cut him off.

"I know and I'm sorry for that. You're the last person I ever wanna hurt," he replied honestly.

"But you keep on doing it so . . ." She looked down and shuffled her feet.

The words that were on pause in her throat would change everything, and although she knew it was for the best that she say them her heart didn't want her to.

"Look," she sighed. "You got a lot going on and I don't wanna be involved anymore so I think it's best we don't hang around each other anymore."

"That's how you feel?" Mills heart cracked.

"You only wanna be bothered wit' me when something's going on wit' you and Jade. I ain't got time for that. And I'm not gon' be puttin' up wit' you gettin' an attitude wit' me every five minutes. I don't have to. Like you said I'm not your girl." Farrah finally looked him in the eye.

"But what if I want you to be?" Mills confessed.

"Let's be honest, Corey. You don't know what you want. But you really need to take the time to figure it out, 'cause I'm at a point now where I need to know are we working toward something, or do you just wanna be friends? If it's friends, then I need to be working on getting' over you," Farrah stated bluntly.

"If I didn't know what I wanted I wouldn't be here."

"Whatever, Mills. Be real." Farrah proceeded to walk past him only for him to grab her arm.

"I ain't no li'l-ass boy. Don't 'whatever' me." Mills made her face him. "Now if we gon' talk let's talk but it ain't gon' be no walking away."

Farrah rolled her eyes, trying her best to seem unaffected by his powerful presence.

"Now I know that things between us have been confusing but I don't lie about how I feel. I'm tired of fakin' and frontin'. I want you and ain't nothin' stopping me from having you."

"Bullshit." Farrah flicked her wrist.

"What you mean bullshit?" Mills drew his head back.

"Niggas lie every day." Farrah arched her eyebrow.

"Don't compare me wit' everybody else. Have I ever lied to you?" He looked her square in the eyes.

"No."

"A'ight, then. Now quit actin' like a spoiled brat and kiss me," he demanded.

Farrah's panties instantly became soaked. Mills had never been so forceful with her. This was the moment she'd dreamt of. For years she'd longed for him to take it there, and now that he was she was scared. Scared that if she gave in what they shared would turn into heartbreak, the kind of heartbreak that would last a lifetime.

"I'm not gon' ask you again," Mills said sternly.

"I don't know, Mills." Farrah held her head down. "I can't." She looked up, choked.

"What? You ain't attracted to me?"

"You a'ight. I've seen better," Farrah toyed with him.

"No, you haven't," Mills said firmly.

Farrah wanted desperately to tell him that in her dreams she'd yearned for him, but now that she was presented with the possibility of having him she feared what might happen afterward. He belonged to someone so he could never be hers. But there he was, ready to make his move. For years Farrah had fought this feeling, but at that moment she was tired of fighting. Every crevice of her body wanted to give in. Her tongue was begging to taste his. All Farrah had to do was give the okay.

Mills stared into her eyes intensely. He could see the fear in her eyes. It was written all over her face. Little did Farrah know, he was scared too, because Mills knew that once he gained access into her honey-coated walls he'd want it again and again and again. He wouldn't be able to resist it anymore. She'd have to be his, but how could she be when he had someone waiting for him at home?

Then Cee Lo's "Bodies" came through the speakers and the mystical beat took a hold of Mills. Suddenly it was the night of his party in Brooklyn all over again. Farrah was there right in front of him, ripe for the picking and begging to be kissed. Unlike the last time when the song played and the military drumbeat, horns, and dimmed lights consumed them, Mills wasn't going to play it safe.

He was tired of pretending that all Farrah was was a friend. Yes, he had a girl and, yes, Farrah was his man's ex, but if he didn't take her into his arms immediately he'd go insane. Before Farrah could get away, Mills forcefully took a handful of her hair and pulled her face toward him.

Caught off guard by his forwardness, Farrah gazed up into his eyes. His brown eyes said it all. He wanted her just as much as she wanted him. Chest to chest, Farrah could feel the stiffness of Mills's hard dick on her thigh as he swept her hair to one side and gently kissed her lips. As their tongues toyed with one another Mills slipped his hand underneath Farrah's shorts and caressed her ass.

Not in the least bit intimidated by his aggressiveness, Farrah ran her small hand up and down the length of his dick. She figured Mills would have a big dick but, damn, his dick reached all the way down to the middle of his muscular thigh. Instead of touching it Farrah wanted to see it, so she unzipped his jeans.

Within a split second both of them had their clothes off. Mills stood naked as Farrah dropped to the floor. His thick ten-inch dick dangled before her begging to be licked. Farrah normally wouldn't have given a man head so soon but with Mills it was different. There was no way around it. She had to do it. Her mouth demanded her to. Hungrily she took him in her mouth. Using her right hand she stroked his shaft.

"Mmm," she moaned, savoring the first taste.

Mills watched on with delight as Farrah greedily devoured his dick. She was a beast at giving head. He thought he dug her before but now she had him wrapped around her finger.

"Damn, girl." He groaned in agony.

Farrah shot him a devilish grin and continued to work her magic. If she could she would stay down there forever. The taste of Mills's cock was addictive.

"Let me see your tongue," Mills demanded.

Farrah happily stuck out her tongue as Mills took his dick and slapped it against her taste buds.

"Get up. I wanna taste that pussy."

Farrah quickly sprang into action by standing up and holding one of her legs in the air. Down below Mills frantically licked Farrah's clit. Farrah didn't know if she was coming or going. The entire room was spinning. Wanting her to reach her ultimate climax, Mills sucked on her clit until she begged him to stop.

"Oooooh, that feels so good." She squirmed. "Mills! Oh my God! I'm gonna cum," she whined. "Shit! Baby!" She rubbed the top of his head. "Stop, I'm gonna cum!"

"You sure you want me to stop?"

"Yes, I wanna cum on your dick," Farrah panted.

Always the one to please Mills forcefully pressed her back up against the wall. As he entered her wet slit Farrah's leg instantly wrapped around his waist. Never taking his eyes off her, Mills ground his hips slowly. He wanted Farrah to feel each thrust and she did.

Mills's dick was spellbinding. She'd never felt anything like it before. It was like his dick was made especially for her. She couldn't catch her breath. His dick was hitting her spine and she loved it. Khalil never hit it like this. He was never concerned with whether or not she was pleased.

Mills, on the hand, handled her body with care. He wasn't going to be pleased unless she was pleased. In the middle of her doorway Farrah and Mills made love for hours. Neither was willing to stop until the other begged for mercy.

Chapter Twelve

Rumor has it she ain't got your love anymore.
—Adele, "Rumor Has It"

With one single kiss on the lips everything in Mills's life changed for the better. He went from being a confused, angry, bitter, and sad man to a man who was excited about life and all of the wonderful possibilities it had to offer. And, it was all because of Farrah; being with her made him feel whole again. She filled a void in him that had been vacant for months.

He enjoyed every waking moment they spent together. She brought laughter back into life, and peace. Nothing with her was dramatic, over the top, or extra. Being with her was easy and she made him feel comfortable enough to be himself, which he appreciated. Day by day, his feelings for her grew more and more. Before he knew it a hint of love had begun to blossom in his heart.

Sitting on the leather bench in front of his bed, Mills tied up his Maison Martin Margiela sneakers. He and Farrah were heading to the Gentleman Jack Art, Beats + Lyrics event. He was already fifteen minutes late picking her up and Farrah, being a stickler for time, was sure to be calling soon. As Mills slipped on his other shoe he heard the unpleasant sound of Jade entering the house.

If anything was gonna put a pep in his step to get moving it was her. Mills couldn't stand being around her. For weeks they'd both done their individual best to avoid one another. After their talk an unspoken war had begun between them. Instead of using guns, missiles, or grenades they used the silent treatment, rolling of the eyes, grunts of displeasure, stomping, and slamming doors as way of attack.

Mills spent as much time away from home as he could. The only time he came home was to shower and change. It seemed like when he was coming in Jade was leaving and vice versa and today would be no different. Anxious to leave Mills stood up and checked himself in the mirror to ensure that his outfit was on point.

Pleased with the way he looked he grabbed his keys and walked down the steps to the door. He could see Jade out of the corner of his eye check-

ing the mail. Normally he would've been excited
to see her. In the past he would've stopped to
appreciate the curves of her frame but now when
he saw her his heart felt nothing but anger and
resentment.

As Jade flipped through a stack of mail she
noticed Mills heading toward the door, dressed
to kill. He looked photo shoot worthy. A pair of
Gucci shades covered his eyes and since it was
cool outside he sported a blue jean button up.
The sleeves were rolled up and the shirt was
unbuttoned and exposed a Blvck Scvle T-shirt
underneath. On his lower half he donned a pair
of light gray fitted jeans.

For weeks Jade had peeped how he hadn't been
at the house much and how he hadn't slept in their
bed. At first she chalked it up to him being in his
feelings and him trying to teach her a lesson but,
knowing the game and how it was played, Jade
quickly realized that Mills was doing more than
teaching her a lesson. He was seeing someone else
and Jade didn't like it one bit.

Sure, she was doing her own thing and had
been doing so for a while but Mills was still hers.
She didn't want to see him with someone else,
at least not until she and Rock were officially
together. "Where you going?" She tossed down
the mail as Mills unlocked the door.

"You talkin' to me?" he asked, shocked.

"Who else would I be talkin' to?" Jade folded her arms across her chest and stood back on her leg.

"Out." Mills pulled the door open.

"So what's going on, Mills?" Jade shouted after him.

"What you talkin' about?" he asked dryly.

"I mean, ever since we got into it and you accused me of cheatin', you been actin' funny."

"I've been actin' funny?" Mills chuckled. "So you fuckin' another nigga and I'm the one actin' funny? You must be crazy."

"No need to call names," Jade spat sarcastically.

"Look you holding me up. To answer your question I'm doin' me. As a matter of fact I'm doin' me so much I been thinkin' about gettin' my own spot."

"What you mean yo' own spot?" Jade furrowed her brows. "What, you call yo'self breakin' up wit' me or something?" Her heart thumped loudly.

"I'm doing what you said. I'm taking the time out to think about whether me and you need to be together."

"That don't mean go and get your own fuckin' place," Jade yelled.

"I'm not about to argue wit' you. I'm late as it is already," Mills responded over the conversation.

"You late to be wit' that bitch?" Jade fumed.

"Like you told me, think what you wanna think." Mills turned to walk out of the door only for Jade to push it shut.

"You . . . ain't . . . going . . . nowhere!"

"Man, you better fall back," Mills warned as his cell phone vibrated.

Mills checked the screen and saw that it was Farrah. He was half an hour late now. Instead of answering, Mills sent her call straight to voice mail. He'd call her back once he got in the car.

"I'm up." He placed his right hand on the knob only for Jade to try to snatch his phone out his left.

"Didn't I just tell yo' ass to fall the fuck back?" He pushed her as his phone vibrated again.

"No, you did not just put your hands on me. Oh, you have lost yo' ever-lovin' mind, nigga!" Jade pushed him back.

"Don't put your hands on me no more, Jade," he warned.

"What you gon' do? Nothin'! I dare you to hit me, nigga." Jade rolled her neck.

"You look real silly right now." Mills looked at her with pure disgust in his eyes.

"Yo' cheatin' ass ain't shit!" Jade shook her head.

"See that's were you got the game fucked up. I don't cheat 'cause I ain't shit. I cheat 'cause you ain't shit," Mills barked.

"So you admit it, you are seeing somebody!"

"Yep." Mills nodded. "I sure in the fuck am and she waiting on me right now so . . . deuces." He threw up the peace sign and walked out of the door.

Stunned by his response, Jade stood unable to speak. She'd really done it this time. She'd pushed Mills too far. Never in a million years did she think he'd seek comfort from another woman and be honest about it. Now what was she to do? She somewhat cared for him but really didn't want him, yet, needed him. Feeling as if each second were her last, as he hopped into his car she yelled from the porch, "Well, fuck you then, nigga!"

Frustrated and exhausted from his unexpected throw down with Jade, Mills knocked on Farrah's door. She was sure to have an attitude because he was an hour late but Mills wasn't beat for her shit either. Seconds later he heard the sound of Farrah's heels click down the wooden stairs. Pissed she unlocked the door and shot him a look that screamed she hated him.

"What's up?" Mills kissed her on the cheek and lightly patted her ass.

Caught off guard Farrah stood silent as she watched his back disappear up the steps. *Is this nigga serious?* she thought, closing the door. Trying her best to keep her cool and not go off, Farrah walked up the steps and entered the living room. With her hands on her hips she watched closely as Mills took a seat on the couch. Closing his eyes he inhaled deep, reopened his eyes, grabbed the DirecTV remote and kicked off his sneakers. Thoroughly confused, Farrah scrunched up her face and said, "What are you doing?"

"We not going, so sit down," Mills said evenly.

"You say what now?" Farrah leaned her head forward as if she hadn't heard him right.

"I don't feel like going no more." Mills kept his focus on the television screen.

"Okayyyyyy." Farrah frowned. "But I thought we had plans."

"We did; now we don't." Mills flipped through the channels.

"Boy, please." Farrah chuckled, snapping her fingers. "You better get yo' life. Do you see what I got on?" She twirled around in a circle.

"Yeah, and it look like yo' feet hurt," Mills joked, looking her up and down.

"Ha-ha-ha funny. No, seriously c'mon, babe, we already late as it is." Farrah tried to pull him up by the arm.

"I said I don't wanna go." He resisted.

"Like, are you for real right now?" Farrah stepped back, becoming upset. "What was the fuckin' point of me even gettin' dressed then!"

"Please don't start a bunch of yellin'." Mills exhaled, emotionally drained. "Just come sit down." He patted his hand on couch.

"Yo," Farrah scoffed, perplexed. "Like . . . I don't even know what to say right now."

"You really wanna go to the party?" Mills questioned, becoming angry all over again. "C'mon let's go." He turned off the television, pissed.

"Are you serious right now?" Farrah asked, shocked by his behavior.

"You wanna go so c'mon let's go!" He grabbed one of his sneakers.

"I wouldn't go wit' you now even if you got on all fours and crawled to that muthafucka!" Farrah snarled.

"Well, then I guess we're not going 'cause ain't no way in hell that's happening," Mills shot back sarcastically.

"You know what I'm gonna do? I'ma go upstairs and when I come back down please be gone." Farrah walked toward the steps, trying her best to remain calm.

"What?" Mills screwed up his face.

"You heard me. Put back on your sneakers and bounce 'cause I do not, and I repeat do not, have time for this shit," Farrah stressed. "You only got one time to send me to voice mail, boo boo, and you late! Nah," she said after a pause. "Got me sittin' up here lookin' like a damn fool waiting on you! While you over there wit' her! No, ma'am." Farrah paced back and forth. "I'm not playin' this game wit' you!" She wagged her index finger back and forth. "No, sir." She shook her head; thinking back on how Khalil treated her in the past.

"What are you talkin' about?" Mills eyed her quizzically.

"This shit ain't going nowhere!" She threw up her arms. "You got a whole bitch at home you been wit' for six years and judging by tonight you still over there tryin' to work shit out wit' her. Which you need to, 'cause y'all belong together. Y'all two confused muthafuckas!" Farrah said, allowing her fears about their so-called relationship to spill to the surface.

"Yo' you trippin'." Mills began to put on his shoes.

"I'm trippin?" Farrah stormed over into his direction. "You sholl right! I should've never started fuckin' wit' you in the first place! You're Khalil's pot'nah! Like no, I'm good! I'm not about to go back to being sad and miserable behind some nigga just because the dick is good! Been there done that and she," Farrah said referring to herself in third person, "is not going back there no more! No matter how much I like you! My heart can't take another heartbreak and you the type of nigga who will kill me!"

Tears formed in Farrah's eyes. "I like you, Mills . . . a lot." She tried her best to stop herself from crying but the tears came rolling down her cheek anyway. "But I wanna be your only one. I have to be first. I can't play second to no one. For once in my life I wanna be loved the way I love everyone else and if I keep on fuckin' wit' you my feelings are gonna get hurt. I can see it." She wiped her face and tried to steady her rapidly beating heart.

"Besides . . . this shit is foul and I don't want no part of it. So let's just"—Farrah found herself unable to breath—"pretend like this shit never happened. You do yo' thing and I'll do mine."

"Whateva, man, if that's what you want that's cool," Mills said hastily. "'Cause both of y'all gettin' on my fuckin' nerves."

"Both of y'all?" Farrah's heart cracked into a million pieces.

"Yeah, you heard me," Mills said, fed up. "Both . . . of . . . y'all . . . are . . . getting . . . on . . . my . . . fuckin' . . . nerves but for two different reasons! Her because I don't wanna be wit' her and she won't let go and you 'cause I'm tryin' to be wit' you but you won't shut the fuck up! I ain't come over here for a bunch of arguing and carrying on! I came over here to sit my black ass down, chill, get me something to eat, and fuck the shit outta you in about an hour! But you so caught up in being scared and tryin' to run that you can't see that I'm tryin' to let this bitch go 'cause I'm tryin' to love you."

"You love me?" Farrah repeated, outdone.

"Yeah, but you gotta stop runnin', Farrah, 'cause I'm only gon' chase you but for so long."

"You're like Tyler Perry right now. You're jokin' but you're not funny." She prayed to God he wasn't playing.

"Real talk, I told her I was moving out tonight," Mills confessed.

Farrah wanted to leap in the air for joy but the fact still remained that he and Jade had been together for six years. There was no way he could just walk away and pretend that what they had didn't exist. Then there was Khalil. He was sure to lose his mind if he ever found out about them.

Too much turmoil would come behind them if they took that leap off the bridge and became one. Farrah had just gone through hell. She didn't intend on going back.

"Whateva, Corey. It really don't matter. It is what is. Me and you can't be together." She tried to convince herself.

"You still on that shit?" Mills shot up from the couch.

"If that's what you wanna call it." Farrah shrugged her shoulders.

"So nothin' I just said mattered to you?" Mills's nostrils flared as he came closer.

"No." Farrah took a step back.

"You don't mean that." Mills inched closer.

"Yes, I do." Farrah's back met with the wall.

"Don't make me fuck you up," Mills warned, standing before her.

Intimidated and turned on by his presence Farrah swallowed hard. His eyes seemed to pierce through to her soul. It wasn't fair how one human being could have so much control over another. In that very moment she wanted to become immersed in his arms but fear kept her at bay. She wanted so much to be his. This was what she'd secretly prayed for but the consequences behind them becoming one would be of biblical proportions.

"What about Khalil?" she whispered, as he slid his hands up her skirt.

"What about the fact that I love you?"Mills peeled her thong down. "I know you love me too." He unbuckled his jeans.

"I do." Farrah moaned as the room began to spin again.

Mills had placed her legs into the crook of his arms and inserted himself deep within. Farrah immediately gasped for air. Mills's dick filled her up to full capacity. It was her kryptonite. She loved it and she hated it. She loved it because the orgasms she got from it sent her on a high but she hated it 'cause she couldn't go a second without yearning for it.

Mills's dick constantly stayed on her mind. Yet she wouldn't have it any other way. Each time they made love they became closer. Mills enjoyed getting Farrah off. The look on her face alone when she came was pleasure enough for him. If he could he would spend every waking moment of his life inside her.

"Goddamn." Farrah's eyes rolled to the back of her head.

The intense electricity in her middle was building with each stroke. An orgasm was building. Farrah loved this part of sex. It always felt like she was a plane gearing up for takeoff. Mills placed his face in the crook of her neck and gripped her ass tight. The nut in the tip of his dick was explosive. The soft moans lingering in the air were turning him on to the fullest.

Mills pressed his palm against the wall and dug in deeper. Her wet walls were devouring his dick. The euphoric feeling couldn't be described. Farrah's nails dug into his back as he drilled a permanent hole in her pussy.

"Mills," she squealed. "Ahhhhhhh! Ahhhhhh-hhhhhhhhhh!"

Her legs had begun to shake.

"Fuck," Mills groaned, feeling his knees buckle.

The faster he pumped the more her titties jiggled. The visual was mesmerizing. There was nothing he didn't want to do to her. There would be no running that night. She was his until the sun came up. Gripping her waist Mills locked eyes with hers. Farrah's torso was easing up and down the wall.

They were both on the brink of climaxing. Then as suddenly as rain began to fall Mills's and Farrah's entire bodies shook and they were transported into space.

Chapter Thirteen

Maybe we movin' too fast but fuck it let's crash.
—Lil Wayne,
"Marvin's Room (Freestyle)"

It was one of those Saturdays where it seemed like everybody in St. Louis was out. The streets were packed with people. Unable to resist an unusually sunny fall day, Farrah and her girls headed to the six-block entertainment and shopping district in St. Louis known as the Delmar Loop. They were going to shop and have lunch.

They'd already hit up boutiques like Tag, Sole and Blues, and Zeizo. Farrah, being the fashionista she was, scooped up two fabulous blouses and three pairs of wedges. For the first time in three years she felt free. Everything in her life was picture perfect. After dealing with Khalil for so long she forgot what peace felt like. She'd forgotten that life didn't have to consist of watching her every word, walking on eggshells, apologizing for someone else's wrongs, never having her feelings validated, and being constantly abused.

With Mills her feelings were just as important as his. He respected her thoughts and ideas. She didn't have to barter for his time and he made it known that any time he spent with her was a blessing. The constant smile on Farrah's face and heart contributed not only to Mills but her change in personality. She demanded more and wasn't willing to settle for anything less. She wasn't willing to tolerate nonsense just for the sake of having a man.

By doing so she learned that she wasn't losing out by sticking to her beliefs but gaining self-confidence. And after praying so long for the right man to come into her life and asking God for discernment she was finally blessed with Mills.

After shopping until their feet hurt and their stomachs growled the girls went to Blue Ocean Sushi for lunch. Blue Ocean Sushi was a quaint family-owned restaurant that served authentic Japanese cuisine. It was one of Farrah's favorite sushi restaurants in St. Louis. Since it was a gorgeous day the girls sat outside in the warm breeze and talked shit while munching on shrimp tempura rolls and crunchy, spicy tuna rolls.

"Y'all going out tonight?" Camden asked before stuffing a roll into her mouth.

"I was thinking about it," Farrah replied, wiping her hands on her napkin.

"Girl, please, she ain't going nowhere." London waved her off. "If Mills call her ass right now she'll ditch us in a hot second wit' her soft ass."

"You are an example of what happens when first cousins marry," Farrah joked, laughing.

"Bitch, you better get yo' life." London snapped her fingers. "Don't hate on me 'cause you fallin' in deep."

"No, I'm not." Farrah couldn't help but blush.

"I would believe you if you could say it with a straight face."

"You do seem happier," Camden added.

"I have no idea what you two are talkin' about." Farrah played coy.

"Yeah, a'ight, bitch." London took a sip of water.

"Real talk." Farrah became serious. "Mills is cool."

"I just bet he is." London couldn't help but giggle. "I be hearing y'all in there fuckin'. He be bustin' it wide open, Camden, you hear me." London raised her hand for a high five.

"Oh, word?" Camden slapped her hand.

"The shit goes on for hours!" London added.

"Y'all gettin' it in like that?" Camden asked, surprised.

"You know what? I hate you and your CW hair." Farrah shot London the middle finger.

"C'mon we gotta get going if we gon' make the movie." She searched her purse for her mirror, trying to change the subject.

"This bitch think she's slick. Look at her trying to change the subject," London said, leaving a tip.

"I am not changing the subject. I like Mills a lot. Hell, I ain't gon' even front, I love him, and so far he's been steppin' up to the plate. I just don't wanna allow myself to trip off it too much 'cause once you do we all know shit starts gettin' fucked up."

"Girl, that man is madly, crazy in love wit' you. I can see it all in his eye."

"He thinks he loves me," Farrah countered.

"Oh, he loves you all right. Trust me." London applied a coat of lip gloss to her lips.

"No, I'm not his type. He just doesn't know it yet."

"Girl, please even you don't believe that lie." London flicked her wrist.

"You really think so?" Farrah asked, hopeful.

"Yes. You said he said he loved you."

"He did but I just figured he was just talkin' shit." Farrah crossed her legs.

"No," Camden interjected, "even I can see that y'all are the new Hov and Bey. All y'all need is a baby Blue to complete the picture."

"You are ignorant." Farrah giggled.

"So you don't wanna have my baby?" Mills said from behind.

"Please tell me he is not standing behind me." Farrah covered her face with her hands.

"Don't cover your face up now." Mills pulled her hands down. "Finish saying what you were saying."

"Where you coming from?" Farrah's face lit up.

"I was riding through and saw you."

"Okay, stalker," she joked.

"Never that. How y'all doing?" Mills spoke to the girls.

"Good," Camden and London spoke in unison.

"I didn't mean to interrupt y'all li'l *Sex and the City* moment but, uh, let me holla at you for a second," Mills said to Farrah in a low and raspy tone.

"I'll be right back," she said to the girls before following him. "What's up?" She looked up into his brown eyes and smiled.

"What the fuck is yo' problem?" He screwed up his face.

"What?" Farrah nervously giggled.

"You know it's been like three days since I last saw you right?"

"Yeah. We've both been busy. Besides I thought we were gonna get together tomorrow." She wrapped her arms around his neck.

"Nah, that ain't gon' work. I need to see you right now." He placed her hand on his hard dick. "Look at what you did. That's some bullshit."

"But we were about to go see a movie," Farrah whined, becoming wet.

"What you need to be doing is seeing about this dick," Mills said playfully.

"You are so nasty."

"Go tell yo' girls you'll get up wit' them later. I want you to come take a ride wit' me."

"You better be glad me and my pussy like you," Farrah teased.

"Like?" Mills screwed up his face. "Y'all love me. Now hurry up." He slapped her on the ass.

Farrah rushed back over to the table. "I'm gettin' ready to go take a ride wit' him." She grabbed her purse.

"See I told you she wasn't shit." London looked at Camden.

"I know." Farrah poked out her bottom lip. "But he's so damn cute and his dick is callin' my name."

"Ugh." Camden pretended to throw up.

"Bye, bitches. Love ya!" Farrah waved over her shoulder.

"Cum for me!" London yelled.

"So where are we going?" Farrah asked, sliding into the passenger seat. The cushy leather seats felt like clouds.

"Just sit back and chill." Mills started the engine and began to drive.

ASAP Rocky's "Palace" was playing as the wind whipped through Farrah's hair. It couldn't have been a better afternoon if she'd dreamt it. The sun was starting to set and an orange hue graced the sky. Mills cruised the streets with ease as he lit a blunt and inhaled the contents. Farrah couldn't take her eyes off of him.

Leaned back in the driver's seat Mills took a toke from the blunt and let the smoke snake from between his lips and evaporate into thin air like magic. Farrah couldn't believe that she'd been depriving herself of someone like him for so long. There was a huge difference between dealing with a boy and a man.

Mills epitomized what a strong black man was all about. He was secure, smart, sexy as hell, and his pretty boy swag was unreal. She felt like a woman with him. Any rules she had were thrown out the window. She was done with guarding her heart. Mills had earned her heart, her soul, and most importantly her trust.

"You have fun wit' yo' homegirls?" He looked at her out of the corner his eye.

"Yeah."

"By the way you look pretty today. I'm diggin' the hippie chic thing you got going on." He massaged her thigh.

"Why thank you." Farrah looked down at her outfit. She was wearing a burgundy fedora, gold necklace, red blouse, red skinny jeans with zipper pockets, Christian Louboutin black suede and leather pumps, a leopard-print cross-body bag, and tons of gold bracelets.

"So you still not gon' tell me where we're going?" she probed.

"Nope."

"You know that this could be considered kidnapping?"

"You want me to kidnap you." Mills chuckled.

"Just a tiny bit." Farrah winked.

"Be careful what you ask for." Mills pulled up to the Central West End section of St. Louis, which was a posh shopping and eating area.

"C'mon." He got out and opened her door.

Her hand in his, they began to take a slow stroll down the street. It was a beautiful day to fall in love. The soft hue from the sun was cascading a warm glow onto their skin. Birds were happily singing. The soothing breeze swept through the atmosphere causing the tree branches to sway in the wind. Farrah couldn't have been more content with her life at that moment. She prayed that it stayed that way forever. She never wanted it to end.

Neither did Mills. His spirits hadn't been this high in a while. At this point no other woman was touching Farrah. He'd been around the world and back but no one compared to her. He could easily see her being his wife. And yes, that was a bold statement to make after only a short while but Mills couldn't deny the way he felt. She was his and he was hers and that was the way it was gonna stay.

"I love this neighborhood." Farrah leaned her head against his arm.

"Me too." Mills wrapped his arm around her neck. "Ay, guess what?" He looked down at her.

"What?" Farrah gazed up into his eyes.

"I met with my agent today and we finalized the deal to open my own skate park."

"That's what's up." Farrah beamed. "I'm so happy for you." She squeezed him tight.

"I'm hella excited."

"I know you are," Farrah replied as they walked though a residential neighborhood.

The houses on the block were exquisite. All of the lawns were immaculate and the families who lived inside of them were so perfect they seemed manufactured.

"So question?" Farrah's mouth became dry. She'd been dreading asking this question for weeks. "What's the deal wit' you and Jade? Are y'all like officially over?"

"Yeah . . . I told you that the night me and you got into it," Mills replied.

"So there's like no chance of y'all working shit out?" Farrah had to confirm.

"Nah, I'm good. Plus how can I work shit out wit' her when I'm in love wit' you?" Mills kissed her on the forehead.

"Aww that's sweet." Farrah beamed from the inside out. "Hey, I never asked"—she tapped Mills on the chest—"do you ever wanna get married?"

"Yeah. I don't wanna be alone. I wanna have somebody to come home to, preferably you if you act right." Mills wrapped his arm around her neck.

"Aww yeah? You would marry me?" She smiled fondly at the thought.

"In a heartbeat."

"Aww," Farrah poked out her bottom lip then kissed him.

"Would you marry me?" Mills asked.

"Is this a proposal?"

"Nah, not yet." He laughed some.

"Booooo." Farrah gave him a thumbs-down.

"Shut up." He tickled her side.

"Stop . . . stop . . . stop." Farrah laughed uncontrollably. "Seriously." She calmed herself down. "Yes, I would marry you."

"Is that a promise?" Mills kissed her lips, rotating between the top and the bottom.

"Yes, that's a promise," Farrah replied, enveloped by his touch.

"Until then let's go back to the crib. All this talk about marriage is making my dick hard."

Chapter Fourteen

Don't dare send me straight to voice
mail. Babe I'm just gon' text you.
      —Jennifer Hudson,
     "No One Gonna Love You"

Bored, Jade lay in the center of the bed with the television on and the volume down low. Elle Varner played while she flipped through the new issue of *Nylon* magazine. She'd been patiently waiting for Rock to call all afternoon. He was supposed to be flying out to see her. They hadn't seen each other in weeks and she was dying to see him in the flesh. She needed to touch him, taste him, and smell his scent. All she'd dreamt of was him holding her in his arms and him whispering in her ear how much he missed her as well.

Now that Mills was gone she was free and clear to see and fuck whomever she pleased. At first, she was upset over Mills leaving and even thought about placing her tail between her legs and saying "I'm sorry" but, Jade being Jade, she quickly changed her mind.

First off, she wasn't the apologetic type. Plus, she had nothing to be sorry about; Mills openly confessed to cheating on her. At least she had the decency to be discreet about her affair. Jade often found herself wondering if the woman he was seeing was Farrah. If it was she was sure to have a fit. It was one thing to cheat but to cheat with someone she knew and had been around was a whole other equation.

Secondly, without Mills being up her ass every five seconds she had all the free time in the world to devote herself to Rock. It felt good not to have to sneak around or hide her feelings for him anymore. Everything she wanted was coming to fruition. She and Rock were closer than ever. At any moment they would officially be together and she could move on with her life for real. While Jade daydreamed about a life outside of St. Louis with Rock, her cell rang.

"Hello?" she answered, realizing it was him calling.

"What you doing?"

"Chillin'. What are you doing?" She smiled so hard her cheeks began to hurt.

"Just walked in the crib," he answered wearily.

"Wait a minute." Jade paused and looked at her watch. "Why aren't you on your way to the airport?"

"I never said I was coming for sure," Rock said casually.

"Weeeeeeell, are you coming or not? 'Cause I'm sittin' here waiting on you."Jade felt her temperature rise.

"I don't know." Rock grunted, sitting down. "I'm tired and my back hurts. I just wanna lie back for a minute. Plus, my homeboy Cruz supposed to be stoppin' by."

Jade swallowed hard and tried her best to control her temper. Whenever Rock got to spitting a bunch of excuses it meant that he was gonna be on some bullshit.

"If you talkin' about lyin' back that mean you ain't coming," she said, about to flip.

"I didn't say that. Even if I don't come tonight I can always come tomorrow," Rock reasoned.

"But that's not what we discussed. You said you were coming today. Now all of a sudden you're tired and your back hurts. Just say what you mean, Rock. Either you're coming or you're not."

"Yo, I said I'd let you know." He raised his voice. "Look." He took a deep breath. "I'm gettin' ready to go take a shower. Once Cruz leave I'll call you and let you know what's up," Rock said, trying to control his anger.

"Okay." Jade rolled her eyes and hung up.

A sinking sensation permeated the pit of her stomach. She couldn't stand when Rock started to act funny. She thought they were past all of the petty bullshit but here he was acting up again. Two hours passed and Rock had yet to pick up the phone and let her know what the deal was. Fed up with waiting for him to call, Jade picked up the phone and called him but, after five rings, the call went to voice mail. Since he didn't pick up she decided to text him.

> To: Rock
> Call me please
> Sent: Sat, Oct 20, 2012

A half hour went by and Jade had gotten no response to her text or a call back.

"Oh, this muthafucka has lost his damn mind," she said out loud as she dialed his number again.

"What's up?" he answered dryly.

Jade could hear the sound of the television and some guys' voices in the background.

"Umm, what you mean what's up? You ain't see me call you and text you?" she asked, barely able to breathe.

"Nah," he lied. "What the text say?"

"I asked you to call me."

"Oh naw, I ain't get that."

"Well, are you coming or not 'cause I'm tired of waiting," Jade quipped.

"Cruz and some of my other pot'nahs are over here and we playin' the game so I'll call you as soon as they leave." Rock tried to end the conversation.

"No!" Jade shot, fed up. "Look, I'm not about to play these silly games wit' you. It's either you coming or you're not."

"Well nah, I'm not," Rock retorted, fed up as well.

Floored by his attitude Jade held the phone speechless. She had no idea why Rock was being so mean to her. Had she committed some kind of crime that she was unaware of? All she remembered was them talking at long length the day before about him visiting her. He'd seemed excited then. Now things were totally different. It wasn't even like she was talking to the same man. Frozen stiff Jade lay on her stomach wondering where and when things had gone wrong and how she could make them right again.

"Hello?" Rock said.

"Yeah," Jade finally uttered. "I'm . . . trying to figure out what the problem is here. Did I do something to you?"

"No, but we are gon' have to talk," Rock finally revealed.

"Talk about what?" Jade quipped, taken aback.

"I think we need to start setting some boundaries between us, 'cause you're starting to expect stuff from me that you shouldn't."

"'Cause I asked you if you were coming or not?" she responded, confused.

Her heart was thumping so loud she could barely concentrate.

"It's a lot of things and I don't really feel like gettin' into it right now. We'll talk about it later," Rock confirmed.

"That's some bullshit, Rock, and you know it." Jade's heart raced. "I haven't done nothin' to you for you to be even coming at me like this. I'm the one who needs to be upset, not you. You played me!"

"See that's what I'm talkin' about. It's always about you and how you feel!" Rock shouted, not caring that he had company.

"You don't take into consideration that I had practice today or that I'm tired! It's all about what you want and since you're not gettin' your way it's a problem. Well, fuck it. Let it be a problem 'cause I'm not about to kiss your ass. That's that nigga you fuck wit' job not mine. Don't come at me wit' that bullshit, straight up."

"And what's that suppose to mean?" Jade's bottom lip trembled.

Rock closed his eyes and took a deep breath and calmed himself down. "It means I'm gettin' ready to get off this phone."

"Are you fuckin' kidding me? Do you got some chick over there?" Jade wished she could see into the phone and into his house.

"No, but if I did what could you say? We're not together!" Rock shot, causing her to lose her breath.

Jade lay silent, unable to even blink. She felt like she'd been stabbed in the heart one million times. "Where is all of this coming from?" Tears stung her eyes.

"Where the fuck you think it's coming from? It's coming from me! Are you retarded?"

"But I haven't done anything to you!" Jade found herself crying like a baby.

"You don't get it, man." Rock ran his hand down the back of his head.

"Get what?" she yelled as tears burned her cheeks.

"I'm about to get off this phone 'cause this conversation is going nowhere." Rock placed his thumb on the end button.

"Rock!" Jade pleaded. If he hung up she was sure to lose her mind.

"I'll call you later, Jade." Rock took the phone away from his ear and ended the call.

"Rock!" Jade shrieked as the phone went dead.

Chapter Fifteen

Are you drunk right now?
—Drake, "Marvin's Room"

"Thank you." Farrah sighed, signing off on another shipment of clothing.

She was elated that her and London's business was growing at a rapid speed but the increase in inventory was overwhelming. With Camden out sick and London always being on London time, Farrah was left to do the majority of the work by herself. She found herself styling clients, packing up one-of-a-kind designer frocks to ship back to fashion houses, opening boxes from designers, hanging the items, doing fittings, answering phones, faxing, printing, and hitting up boutiques to pull pieces all by herself.

She was mentally and physically drained. The fact that it was her birthday and she was working much too hard didn't make it any better. She'd planned on having a nice, relaxing day at the spa where she would get her hair done, get a facial, massage, manicure, and pedicure but, no, she was stuck in their office unpacking boxes.

No one besides her mother had called to say happy birthday. Not even Mills had called, which pissed her off to the fullest extent. They'd been kicking it tough for over a month and she'd spoken about her birthday every five minutes, so how he'd forgotten was beyond her. But maybe she was expecting too much from him. It wasn't like he'd made her his girl.

Yes, he'd told her he loved her and they spent every waking moment with one another. He'd wined and dined her and had even bought her a few lavish gifts but still the words, "You're mine," hadn't slipped through his lips. As a sweat bead trickled down Farrah's forehead, she realized that she'd reached her breaking point. There was no way in hell she was going to finish unpacking and sorting the contents of twelve boxes by herself. Overwhelmed, she called London.

"Hello?" London answered with a slight giggle.

"I'm glad to hear you're having fun. Where are you?" Farrah said, fanning herself with her hand.

"I'm on the way, girl." London laughed. "Stop," she whined.

"Oh my God! Are you still wit' Teddy?" Farrah hissed.

"Yeah, but I swear I'm gettin' ready to get up now."

"So you ain't even dressed yet?" Farrah fumed.

"It'll only take me like ten minutes to shower and slip on some clothes," London swore.

"No, it won't, London. Do you realize that the showroom is a mess? Better yet, do you even realize that it's my birthday?" Farrah finally snapped.

"Aww, my bad. Damn it is, ain't it? Happy birthday, doll face. What you at the office for? You better enjoy your day."

Farrah scoffed and held the phone, stunned. London just didn't get it. If Farrah didn't work her ass off nothing would get done.

"Bye, London." Farrah placed her thumb on the end button.

"What? You mad?"

"Yes, I am mad. It's my fuckin' birthday and I'm workin'. I'm hot and I'm sweaty and I'm pissed off. I can barely walk in here there's so much crap!" Farrah kicked a box. "All week I've been handling this shit by myself while you're off bullshittin' around and it's not right! It's not fair. And do you know that muthafucka hasn't even called me and said hello let alone happy birthday?" she said, referring to Mills.

"I knew it was more to the story," London responded.

"Oh no, sweetie, don't get it twisted. I'm mad at you too so take several seats. You suppose to me my best friend and you didn't even remember my birthday. And on the real, London, I'm sick of feeling like I'm running this business by myself. It seem like all you wanna do is run in behind dick. So you know what? Don't even bother coming. Stay over there wit' Teddy. I'll continue to do it by myself," Farrah spat, hanging up.

Normally she would feel bad for going off on her like that, but London had that coming. She'd been slacking off way too much lately. If a dick or some cash wasn't dangling in her face then the chick wasn't motivated. Irritated beyond belief, Farrah closed her eyes and took a deep breath. Homegirl was on twenty and she needed to bring her temper down to at least ten in order to function.

Somewhat calm, she placed six pairs of Jimmy Choos on the shoe wall, then hung three Givenchy gowns on one of the gown racks according to color. Just as she was about to sort through another box her cell phone rang. Beyoncé's "Miss You" ringtone let her know it was Mills. *About time,* she thought, relieved. Half of the day had gone by without even a single text from him. If he would've forgotten her birthday she would've never forgiven him.

"Hi." She smiled for the first time that day.

"What's up, pretty girl? What you doing?"

She frowned. "At the studio unpacking boxes unfortunately."

"Sucks for you but, ay, I need you to do me a favor," Mills responded.

"What?" Farrah immediately became agitated.

"I need you to run over to my hotel room and pick up the blueprints for my skate park."

"Are you serious?" Farrah's heart deflated.

"Yeah, I'm gettin' ready to meet wit' the landscaper in like thirty minutes and I don't have enough time to double back. You gon' do it for me?"

"No!" Farrah said, enraged.

"Why not?"

"'Cause I'm over here up to my neck in shit! I'm tired, I'm hungry, and I honestly just wanna go somewhere and lie down and never talk to none of y'all ever again in life!"

"What I do?" Mills quizzed, put off by her attitude.

"The fact that you even have to ask me that says it all. Bye, Corey." Farrah hung up on him.

Not even a second later Mills called her back, but Farrah didn't bother to pick up.

"I can't believe this muthafucka gon' forget my birthday and then have the nerve to ask me to go on a scavenger hunt for his ass like I'm his goddamn assistant! Nigga, please! Fuck that shit." She spoke out loud to herself as her phone rang again.

"What?" she shrilled, answering his call.

"Damn who pissed in your cereal this morning?" Mills joked.

"What is it, Mills? I don't have time for a bunch of nonsense today." Farrah trembled she was so angry.

"For real, I need you to handle that for me. I wouldn't be asking if it wasn't important. C'mon, pretty girl, do this for me please. I need you."

Unable to resist the sound of a man begging, Farrah caved in and said, "Okay."

"That's what's up! Thanks, babe. I got you, I promise," Mills pledged.

"Mmm hmm, whatever." She rolled her eyes.

"You still got my room key don't you?"

"Yeah."

"Cool. The blueprints are on the table."

"A'ight."

"And can you kinda hurry up? 'Cause we both know you move kinda slow," Mills said sarcastically.

"Mills." Farrah stressed his name, letting him know he was getting on her nerves.

"I'm just sayin'."

"Bye!" She hung up, annoyed.

Farrah placed her red Hermès bag in the crook of her arm and took out her car keys. Forty-five minutes later she was in front of the building Mills asked her to meet him at. He stood in front of the entrance doors looking like a *GQ* model. Mills rocked a pair of black Wayfarer shades, army-green T-shirt, blue jean jacket, indigo-colored jeans, and Bathing Ape railroad boots. *Why he gotta be so damn fine?* Farrah thought, hopping out of her Jeep.

"Here." She slapped the blueprints in his hand.

"What took you so long? The meeting is almost over," Mills said, visibly upset.

"Muthafucka, 'cause it's after five o'clock and I was stuck in traffic!" Farrah spat.

"I'm just sayin' you holding me up."

"You know what?" Farrah held up her hand as if to say freeze. "Let me go before I end up sayin' something I'm gon' regret."

"Nah, hold up." Mills pulled her back.

"No, Mills, let me go!" Farrah yanked her arm away. "It's my fuckin' birthday and you got me runnin' errands like I'm a cast member of *The Help!*"

"Damn it is your birthday. I thought I was forgetting something. Happy birthday, babe." He hugged her but she stood stiffly with her arms down by her side.

"Don't be like that. I'm sorry." He kissed her on the lips. "I promise I'ma make it up to you. Just come up here wit' me real quick so you can meet the landscaper."

"Do it look like I wanna meet a goddamn landscaper?" Farrah looked at him like he was stupid.

"No, but do it for me." Mills hit her with the sad puppy-dog face.

"I just wanna go home." Farrah felt herself on the verge of tears.

"Please, babe, it'll only be a second. Then I promise we can go back to your crib and get in bed together."

Farrah rolled her eyes to the sky.

"Okay, but make it quick. I don't got all day."

"You the shit, you know that." Mills kissed her on the cheek and led her into the building.

"Where are we anyway?" Farrah asked as they boarded the elevator and got off.

"You ask too many questions." He pulled her to what looked like a loft door and knocked.

"I just wanna lie down." Farrah pouted as the door opened and everyone inside screamed surprise.

Floored, Farrah's mouth dropped open. Everyone she loved was there: London, Camden, and Teddy. With her back pressed up against Mills's chest and his right arm wrapped around her waist they stepped inside the loft. Pink paper lanterns and pink balloons hung from the ceiling. In the center of the room was a table set for five. Four small bouquets of pink roses surrounded a pink and white polka-dot cake. Everything was pink from the napkins to the silverware. She even had pink champagne, cotton candy, macaroons, popcorn, and cupcakes.

"I thought you all had forgotten," Farrah cried. "And I thought you were sick!" She hit Camden on the arm.

"I am but I wouldn't miss this for the world."

"Thanks, love." Farrah hugged her. "Eww, but don't get me sick." She quickly let go.

"And you, bitch." Farrah pushed London. "I swear to God I was gon' kill you."

"You know I got you, boo." London squeezed her tight.

"I'm sorry for being so mean."

"You don't know no better." London laughed.

"Hey, Teddy." Farrah waved.

"What up, baby girl. Happy birthday." He hugged her too.

"This is amazing." Farrah stood in the center of the room in awe. "Hold up, whose place is this?"

"Mine," Mills announced from behind.

"When did this happen?" Farrah spun around.

"I signed off on it early this week."

"And you did all of this for me?" Tears formed in Farrah's eyes.

"You know I would do anything for you."

"I feel horrible. I thought that you didn't even care." She leaped into his awaiting arms.

"I would never forget your birthday." Mills kissed her softly on the lips.

"I love you," Farrah whispered low so only he could hear.

"I love you, too."

For the next few hours Farrah and her friends stuffed themselves. Mills had a chef come in and prepare all of Farrah's favorite food. They ate pot stickers, sushi, pasta, and fried shrimp. For dessert they ate red velvet cake and sipped champagne. Farrah ate and laughed so much her stomach ached.

After everyone left she and Mills sat alone on the wooden floor while Coultrain's *The Adventures of Seymour Liberty* album serenaded them. Sweet, soulful sounds from the St. Louis native filled the entire room. It couldn't have been a better setting. Two lovers reveling in each other's touches, kisses, and words while the city skyline watched.

"Did you have fun?" Mills ran his fingers through her hair.

"Yes." Farrah lovingly kissed the palm of his hand.

"I surprised yo' ass, didn't I?" Mills laughed.

"Yeah." Farrah laughed too. "You got me."

"You know you're pretty when you laugh. Your whole face lights up." He ran his index finger down the side of her face.

"Stop, you're making me blush." Farrah covered her face with her hands.

"Stop that." Mills pulled her hands down. "Don't ever hide that pretty face."

"You know all the compliments aren't necessary. I'ma give you some tonight," Farrah joked.

"Shut up." Mills chuckled. "I got you something." He got up and walked toward the back.

"Babe, you didn't have to get me anything. The party was enough." She took a small sip of champagne.

"See that's why I like you. You don't ask for much yet deserve the world." He sat back down in front of her with three gifts in his hands.

"You must be tryin' to get me to suck it tonight," Farrah taunted him.

"I just want you to bounce on it. Now here, open this." He handed her the first gift.

Farrah excitedly tore off the pink wrapping paper and found a box with the words Christian Louboutin written on the top.

"Shut the front door!" she gasped.

Inside were the Bollywoody suede pumps that featured metallic embroidery and multicolor crystals. Being a stylist, Farrah knew that the heels were ultra expensive.

"Mills, I can't accept this. These shoes are almost $3,000."

"You can accept them and you will. There is no return policy over here."

"This is too much." Farrah quickly tried them on. "These are sickening! I'ma about to shut it down in these muthafuckas! Watch out, bitches," she exclaimed.

"Okay, second box." Mills handed it to her.

Farrah opened it and found a butterfly-print cap-sleeve Alexander McQueen dress.

"Boy, you might get some head and some ass tonight! Thanks, baby." She leaned forward for a kiss but Mills stopped her.

"Before you do that I need you to open this first." He handed her the last gift.

Farrah unwrapped the gift and found a box full of white tissue paper.

"There's nothing in here." She looked at him, confused.

"Keep digging."

Farrah continued to sift through the tissue paper and found a key taped to the bottom of the box.

"What is this?" She held it up.

"It's the key to my place. I want you to stay wit' me."

"But—"

"Ain't no but," Mills cut her off. "I like kickin' it wit' you over your crib but yo' girl always there and I be wanting to get loose and I can't. I figured here we'd get to enjoy each other the right way." Mills looked into her eyes. "Look I don't wanna do nothing but wake up to you. I like being around you, Farrah, and when I'm not . . . I'm not right."

All of her life Farrah had waited for a fairytale moment like this to occur. There, before her, sat a man who genuinely adored everything about her and made her feel higher than the sun. When he looked into her eyes she felt loved. Not the superficial here today, gone tomorrow kind of love, but the everlasting love that made you realize there was truly a God.

"I wanna wake up to you too." Farrah kissed him passionately.

Tears filled her eyes to the point she couldn't see. The way she loved Mills couldn't even be described with words. She no longer cared about Khalil's feelings, or anyone else's for that matter. She was doing her and she was beyond a place of happy.

She was over worrying about whether he would change his mind about them. Every day he made it clear that with her was where he wanted to be. She and Mills were one now. As their bodies intertwined and they climaxed so hard the world quaked, Farrah knew that what they had would last forever.

After making love for what seemed like an eternity, Mills and Farrah lay engulfed in each other's arms. A dim light from the moon softly lit the bedroom. They were both in a deep sleep, but the sound of Farrah's cell phone ringing woke them up.

"Turn that shit off," Mills groaned, rolling over onto his stomach.

"I'm sorry, babe. Go back to sleep." Farrah got up and reached out for her phone. *What the hell does he want?* she thought, gazing at the screen before answering. "Hello?" she said groggily, tiptoeing into the hallway.

But instead of hearing a voice she was hit with loud background noise, which consisted of music and people talking.

"Hello?" Farrah repeated.

Khalil held the phone nervously. Since his first drink he'd pondered calling her. But he couldn't figure out the right words to convey what he felt inside. They hadn't talked in months but the sweet sound of her voice sent chills through his veins. He missed the hell outta her and the large amount of alcohol that he'd consumed in the last few hours only intensified his feelings.

"You 'sleep?" he finally said.

"Yeah." Farrah peeked into the bedroom to ensure that Mills had fallen back to sleep. He had.

"I ain't mean to wake you up! I just wanted to tell you happy birthday!"

"Thanks." Farrah rested her head on the wall. Her body had suddenly become tense. Hearing from Khalil was the last thing she'd expected.

"What you doing? Wake yo' ass up! I know yo' ass ain't 'sleep! It's yo' muthafuckin' birthday! Come out and kick it wit' me!" Khalil exclaimed.

"Are you drunk right now?" Farrah said low into the phone.

"A li'l bit!" He held his head. The room was beginning spin and he was starting to see double. "Baby?" Khalil called out for her.

"What is it?" Farrah asked wryly.

"Can I come . . . Let me come see you for a minute!"

"I'm not at home." Farrah closed her eyes.

"Where you at?"

"Why don't you just go home and go to bed," Farrah suggested.

"Fuck that! Where you at! I know you ain't wit' some nigga!" Khalil shouted.

This was the shit that Farrah didn't miss. When they were together and Khalil got this drunk he'd normally come home and start a fight, then break something.

"I'll talk to you later, Khalil." She tried to get off the phone.

"Farrah! Wait!" he pleaded. "You fuckin' wit' somebody?"

"Yes," she answered, incensed.

"That's fucked up! That's hella fucked up! But I don't even give a fuck." Khalil took a gulp of his drink. "Fuck that nigga! I know you still love me! You still love me don't you?"

"I'm going back to bed. I suggest you do the same." Farrah abruptly ended the call and held the phone close to her chest.

Breathing heavily, she pushed herself off the wall and returned to bed. Mills was in such a deep slumber that he hadn't heard a thing. Farrah curled up beside him. For some reason she felt a little guilty for even answering her phone, like she'd betrayed Mills. But she hadn't. Her life with Khalil was over and she planned on keeping it that way.

Chapter Sixteen

As I lay restless waiting on my phone to ring. Never did ring, never did.
—Stacy Barthe, "Never Did"

It was now or never for Jade. It was time for her to put her pride to the side, stop playin' games, and tell Rock exactly how she felt. There was no way in hell she was going to lose out on not one but two multi-millionaires. And yes, she was throwing caution to the wind by hopping on a flight to L.A. in hopes that Rock would finally give in and be her man, but she was there, and there was no turning back now.

Her plan had to work. She'd planned the whole thing out in her head on the plane. She'd show up at his door and say surprise and he'd be super excited to see her, take her into his arms, and kiss her passionately on the lips. They'd have animalistic, tear each other apart-type sex, she'd tell him how much she loved him and wanted nothing more on earth than to be his girl, he'd say that he wanted the same, and from then on they'd be one.

And sure, since he went off on her for no reason he'd been acting hella funny. He'd suddenly forgotten her number, and when she called him he seemed distant and slightly annoyed by her, but Jade couldn't focus on that. Her heart wouldn't allow her to, although her mind kept telling her repeatedly that something was up. Rock's attitude had switched up unexpectedly. She hadn't changed. If anything, her feelings had intensified.

As the driver pulled up to Rock's luxury apartment building, Jade checked her makeup and teeth in the mirror. As usual, she was flawless. With her heart tucked safely away under lock and key she grabbed her red Birkin bag and hopped out of the back of the Lincoln Navigator. While she smoothed down her dress, the driver grabbed her Louis Vuitton luggage out of the trunk of the car.

Okay, girl, here we go, she thought, walking inside his building. The front desk would have her bags sent up by the doorman. Dressed to kill in a gorgeous metallic tweed Theyskens' Theory dress, Jade knocked on Rock's door.

"Who is it?" he yelled.

"It's me." Jade's voice quivered.

Rock opened the door and looked at her with a surprised and confused expression on his face.

"Surprise!" Jade threw her arms up in the air then hugged him.

"What are you doing here?" Rock asked instead of hugging her back.

"Well, since you wouldn't come to me I decided I'd come to you. Now are you gonna let me in?" She arched her eyebrow.

Rock stepped to the side so she could get past him.

"Aren't you happy to see me?" Jade looked around his place trying to find evidence of another woman, but she found none. The only thing she found was an immaculate and tastefully decorated high-rise apartment that overlooked the city of L.A.

"I guess . . . I mean I wish you would've called first." Rock closed the door behind them.

"Then it wouldn't have been a surprise now would it? Besides I did call you but you didn't answer the phone as usual." Jade turned from side-to-side like a little girl.

"I've been busy," Rock said, flushing in distress.

"Too busy for me?" Jade poked out her bottom lip and entered his personal space. "You didn't miss us." She referred to her vagina while wrapping her arms around Rock's neck.

"Be serious right now, Jade." He fumed, pulling her arms down.

"I'm being very serious. Things between us have been a little shaky lately and I just figured if I came to L.A. we'd be able to set things straight." She traced the outline of his jaw with her index finger.

"Will you stop?" He smacked her hand away.

"Geez." She massaged her hand.

"My bad, I ain't mean to do that," Rock quickly apologized. "It's just . . . I feel what you saying but you just showing up here without my permission ain't cool."

"I didn't think you would mind." Jade felt the air in her lungs slip away.

"Well yeah, I do." Rock picked up his gym bag. "I thought you realized after our last conversation that I needed space."

"And I gave you some space. I guess not enough though." Jade bit the inside of her lip so she wouldn't cry.

"I gotta head to practice so uh . . ." Rock lingered at the door for a minute hoping she'd get the hint, but she didn't. Jade just stood silently staring at him.

"I can't deal with this right now. I'll holla at you later." He slammed the door behind him.

Alone, Jade sat on the back of his couch. The silence surrounding her was deafening. This wasn't how she'd pictured things going down. How could she have read this so wrong? She knew things between them were strained but damn! Rock was acting like she was the last bitch on earth he wanted to see.

Jade wasn't used to this part of the game. She wasn't used to getting her feelings hurt. She was used to being emotionless, but now the tables had turned and she was wide open. Rock was the one thing she couldn't have. No matter what she did he wouldn't give in to her desires, and the more he backed away the more she craved him. He was the forbidden fruit she longed for and she'd come too far to give up now.

After a strenuous practice Rock returned home expecting to find Jade gone, but instead found her in his kitchen with an apron on, fixing dinner. *Is this chick crazy?* he thought, placing down his keys. "What are you still doing here?" he asked, slightly disturbed.

"I knew after practice you'd be starving so I fixed your favorite fried chicken, macaroni and cheese, and sweet potatoes." Jade wiped her hands on the apron. "So go and wash up so we can eat." She shot him a mechanical smile.

A look of horror and disbelief was written all over Rock's face as he set his bag down and headed to the bathroom. Jade wasn't getting it. He needed space. A moment to breathe and gather his thoughts. The more she pushed the more he felt suffocated.

Once his hands were washed he entered the dining room. Candles had been lit and the soulful sound of Stacy Barthe played. Rock kind of felt bad for Jade. She'd gone through all of this trouble to show him how much she cared for him but he honestly couldn't care less. He wasn't really into her anymore. He'd thought his actions showed that but he apparently hadn't made that clear enough.

"The food looks good," he said, placing his napkin on his lap.

"Thanks. I hope you like it." Jade sat down next to him.

After saying grace Rock bit into the crispy chicken and his taste buds danced. "Mmm." He wiped his mouth with his napkin. "Damn that's fire."

"You really like it?" Jade's heart skipped a beat.

"I can't even front, you did yo' thang." Rock took another bite, then abruptly stopped chewing. "You didn't poison this did you?"

"No." Jade waved him off. "Why would you say something like that, silly?" She grinned.

'Cause you're nuts, Rock thought, continuing to eat.

"I'm just happy you're happy." She reached out and caressed the back of his hand.

Rock's body instantly tensed up upon her touch and Jade could feel it.

"Speaking of happiness." She quickly removed her hand. "The reason I flew all the way out here was to tell you that I really care about you, Rock. And I know when this thing between us began it was only supposed to be a momentary thing but here we are a year later. My relationship wit' Mills is over—"

"Jade," Rock tried to speak.

"No, let me finish, 'cause if I don't say it now I never will." She inhaled deep. "Me and Mills are done and I know you don't want to be in a relationship because of all the drama you and your ex-wife went through but I swear to you, Rock, I will never hurt you. I love you," she finally confessed. "And I wanna be wit' you."

"Jade," Rock said, losing his appetite. "We already discussed this."

"I know we did but I want more. I want you to be mine. I want us to be committed 'cause, believe it or not, I already am. I wanna move out here with you and really try to give this thing a go."

"I don't know what to say." Rock rubbed his eyes.

"Just say that you'll think about it," Jade said simply.

Rock didn't have the heart to tell her, but there was nothing to talk about. He'd already made up his mind. He cared for Jade but she wasn't the one for him.

"A'ight, I'll think about it," he lied so she wouldn't continue with the conversation.

The rest of dinner was met with small talk and silence. Rock showered while she cleaned up the kitchen and put the leftovers in the fridge. It was apparent that Jade had no intention of leaving so he sucked it up and played host.

Dying to become immersed in his touch, Jade stripped down to nothing and joined him in the bed. She didn't want much, just for him to satisfy the craving that consumed her loins. By the look in his eyes she could tell he wasn't into it, but she couldn't stop herself. She had to have him anyway she could get him. A piece of him was better than nothing. For weeks all she'd wanted was for him to be by her side. Now they were face-to-face and Jade wasn't going to stop until the spark they once shared was relit.

Straddling him, she leaned forward and tried to kiss him on the lips, but Rock turned his face and the kiss landed on his cheek. Before Jade knew it she was on her back and he'd entered her. Foreplay wasn't even a part of the equation. As he stroked her middle roughly, Rock wouldn't even look Jade in the eye.

Nothing about their lovemaking was magical or tantalizing like in the past. It was strictly sex, nothing more, nothing less. Never before had Jade been made to feel like an empty hole to fill. It was sad because although she knew the dynamics of their relationship had changed drastically, she would rather be there with him then be apart.

Minutes later Rock came, and unlike all the times before, instead of holding her he simply pulled out and went to sleep. Jade pulled the covers up over her naked body and stared at the ceiling. There in the dark salty tears slid from the corners of her eyes. If she had been alone she would have wailed but she wasn't going to dare let Rock see her in such a vulnerable state. She'd already cried over the phone. No, Jade would sulk in silence and try to figure out how to ease her way back into his heart, because she'd reached the point where there was no living without him.

The weekend was finally over and it was time for Jade to return home. She didn't want to leave because she feared that once she left she'd never be able to return again. All weekend Rock had made her feel less than welcome. He made her feel like dirt. All of their conversations were forced and when they had sex he seemed disconnected, like he wasn't even mentally there. He wouldn't even kiss her on the lips. With each second that passed she felt him slip away.

"Your car is here!" he yelled.

"All right, here I come." Jade took one last look at herself in the mirror, then headed toward the door.

"Be safe." Rock gave her a one-armed hug.

"Bye," Jade said awkwardly.

"I'll call you later," Rock assured her.

"Okay," Jade replied, feeling a glimmer of hope.

Sitting in the back seat of the Navigator with her Chanel shades covering her eyes, Jade gazed blankly out of the window. She was at her wit's end. Her life was spiraling out of control. She'd gambled and lost it all. Mills was gone and the man she wanted more than the air she breathed didn't want anything to do with her. Just as she was about to give up and surrender to her circumstances her cell phone rang. A bright smiled crossed her face. It was Rock calling. *Maybe our weekend went better than I thought,* she thought, answering the phone.

"Hello?" she sang.

"Hey." He spoke lightly.

"Hey . . . You miss me already? I can turn around if you want me to." She sat up straight.

"Ay, umm, we need to talk," Rock uttered.

Jade's heart stopped beating. *No, no, no, no, no, no, no.* She cringed. Whenever someone began a conversation with "we need to talk," bad news was right around the corner.

"What's up?" She played it cool.

"I care about you, I do, but I think we may need to fall back from one another for a while," Rock admitted.

"What you mean 'we'? I don't wanna fall back, you do," Jade said at once.

"Listen you deserve a white dress and a happy ending. I'm just not the man to give it to you."

"Where is all of this coming from?" Jade replied, feeling like she was drowning.

"It's just too much and I'm not feelin' it. Plus . . . me and Mya tryin' to work things out."

"So that's what this shit is about!" Jade shot, outraged. "You don't wanna be in a relationship wit' me 'cause you still hung up on that bitch!"

"Watch your mouth, that's my son's mother," Rock warned.

"And? What's that supposed to mean to me?" Jade challenged. "Rock, when you call me, my whole world stop! Everything that you want I give you. You have all of me and now you wanna tell me that you wanna do something different? What kind of shit is that? If this was what you wanted you could've said that from the beginning!"

"I did!" Rock stressed.

"No, you said you didn't want to be in a relationship! But no, it's not that you didn't want to be in a relationship, it's that you didn't want to be in a relationship with me!"

"It's complicated, man."

"Complicated my ass! I sat there and poured my heart out to you all weekend and you just sat there and let me make a fool outta myself!" Her voice quivered. Tears were forming in her throat. "I left my man at home for you!"

"I never told you to do that," Rock barked. "You did that 'cause you wanted to. I told you from the jump what it was so that's on you. You ain't gon' put that shit off on me."

"Wow . . . I cannot believe this shit," Jade scoffed.

"Believe it." Rock hung up before she could say another word.

"No, this muthafucka did not hang up on me," Jade said out loud as she called him back.

But Rock wouldn't answer.

"This is not fuckin' happening," she cried. "This is not happening."

Chapter Seventeen

**Talk if you need to but I can't stay to hear
you, that's the wrong thing to do.**
                    —Drake, "Doing it Wrong"

It'd been weeks since Mills had last stepped
foot inside his and Jade's house. He'd done
everything in his power to avoid her. But he had
a few more things to pick up, so running into her
was inevitable. Upon walking into the house he
noticed that all of the lights were out. *Maybe she
ain't here,* he thought, walking up the steps to
what used to be their bedroom. When he turned
on the lights he was shocked to see her lying in
bed underneath the covers. He wouldn't have
normally tripped off of it, if it hadn't been five
o'clock in the afternoon.

"Jade," he called out.

"What?" she mumbled.

"What's wrong wit' you? You sick?" He looked
around the room, concerned. Balled-up tissue

was everywhere. An empty pizza box and a bottle of vodka were thrown on the floor. Jade hadn't left her room in days. All she'd done was cry and call Rock repeatedly, but he couldn't even be bothered to answer her calls. For some reason he didn't understand that to her he was like a vital organ, she needed him in order to function.

There was no way they could be over. They'd shared too much and put too much energy into it for it to just die so suddenly. When she'd tried to push him away he'd always come back and demanded a space in her life, so why was it that when she tried to do the same thing he was shutting her out?

She couldn't figure out for the life of her where things between them went wrong. All she wanted was for things to go back to the way they had been. She loved him too much to say good-bye. He was all she thought about. Nothing and no one could compare to him. Rock was it for her and she was determined to make him see it.

Sure, he and Mya had history and shared a son, but none of that mattered to Jade. In her mind Mya didn't hold a candle to her. He'd left her for a reason. They'd found in each other what they couldn't with Mills and Mya. They were beyond compatible. They were cut from the same cloth. And yes, she felt stupid for calling him so much but she couldn't stop herself.

If she gave up now they'd be done for good and she'd forever feel like a corpse. The only thing that soothed her was the bottle of vodka. It helped dull the sick feeling in the pit of her stomach that kept her up at night. But she couldn't tell Mills any of this. He'd moved on and was obviously happy while she lay miserable.

"No." She blew her nose.

"What's wrong then?" Mills opened the blinds.

Instead of responding Jade continued to cry and gather her thoughts. She hadn't expected for Mills to make an impromptu visit, but she would use the depressed state she was in to her advantage. She would make it seem like she'd been crying over him, when really her tears were reserved for Rock.

Until she could find a way back into his heart she had to secure her future one way or another. Jade had little to no work experience and without Mills or Rock in her corner she wouldn't be able to survive. Thankfully, Mills had continued to pay the bills at their house, but Jade knew that sooner or later that would cease. Using her pain as a driving force for the performance of a lifetime, Jade lifted the covers from over her face.

Mills tried his best not to feel anything, but her red, swollen eyes, puffy face, and tear-stained face kind of fucked him up. "What you cryin' for?"

"It's nothing." She got up and went into the bathroom to wash her face.

Perplexed by her mood, Mills found a bag and gathered the things he'd come for. "Ay yo." He tapped on the bathroom door once he was done. "I'm about to head out. I hope you feel better."

Jade dried her face and stepped back into the bedroom. "Can I uh . . . talk to you for a second?" She sniffled.

"What's up?" Mills set the bag down.

"I've been wanting to call you and talk to you but I didn't know if you would be willing to talk to me after the way I treated you." Jade held on to the sleeves of her cardigan. "I know I've been a bitch to you and I'm sorry for that. I was just going through something at the time but my intentions were never to push you away.

"I never cheated on you, Mills." Jade tried to sound as sincere as possible. "I swear to God. I would never do that to you. And I know you've moved out and got your own place but I miss you. I know I fucked up but I want you back. I want us back. I don't know when we stopped being us—"

"We stopped being us when you started fuckin' somebody else," Mills shot.

Usually Jade would've gone off, but she had to keep her act up so she played it cool. "I can understand why you think I was seeing somebody else, 'cause I was acting crazy. I wasn't myself. But on everything I wasn't fuckin' around on you. We've been together too long to just give up now."

"I feel what you sayin' but . . ." Mills hung his head.

"And I know you're seeing somebody else and I don't blame you. I just had to let you know how I felt though."

"I just came over here to pick up my stuff. I wasn't expecting all of this," Mills admitted.

"I know and I'm sorry for just springing all of this on you but its how I feel." Jade mustered up some more tears.

Mills wanted to feel sorry for her but she'd done this to herself. He'd tried to hold on to their relationship. He'd given it his all. Now there she stood with tears the size of raindrops rolling down her face.

"I just want you to give me another chance." Jade sobbed.

Mills stared into her eyes. He could see that she badly wanted him to hold her and tell her things would be okay, but he couldn't. The emotions and words that she desired weren't there, and if he told her anything different it would be a lie.

"I gotta go." Mills collected his things.

"Okay, but can we at least get together one day this week and talk if you're not busy?" Jade responded eagerly.

"I can't make you any promises."

"I understand."

"Peace out." Mills left, dumbfounded.

The entire ride home he couldn't take his mind off Jade's revelation. Never in a million years would he have expected her to come at him like that. When he left she seemed pleased, like she was relieved that he would be out of her hair. She didn't try to stop him. She didn't pick up the phone to call him. He'd come to grips with the fact that things between them were over.

Sometimes he thought about her. He wondered where she was at and who she was wit' and if she was thinking about him too. He wondered if she felt any regret for destroying their relationship. But almost two months had gone by and he hadn't heard a word, so he blocked her out of his mind and went on with life. Instead of focusing on Jade and the misery she brought into his life, he focused his attention on Farrah.

She'd picked up the shattered pieces left of his heart and mended it with prayer, words of encouragement, and unwavering love. The love they shared was the kind of love movies were made of. With Farrah it was smooth sailing. The more time they spent together the more he began to feel like himself again. But he'd felt the same way with Jade once upon time.

To this day he had no physical proof of her cheating, just a gut intuition. So, what if he was wrong? What if he'd overreacted and given up too soon? It was all too much to process and Mills's head was beginning to hurt. Back home he parked his car in the garage, boarded the elevator, and got off on his floor.

"Hey, babe." Farrah spoke from the couch as he entered. A cashmere blanket was draped over her body as she watched the Syfy network's hit show *Face Off*. After an easy day at work she found herself unusually exhausted and needing to lie down.

"Hey, pretty girl." Mills walked over and kissed her.

"How did everything go? Jade ain't cause you no problems did she?"

"Uh nah," Mills stammered. "She wasn't even there," he lied. *Why the fuck did you just lie?* he thought.

"Well that's good. No drama for you today," Farrah said with enthusiasm.

"Yeah." Mills pretended to chuckle.

"What are you about to do?" Farrah questioned.

"Put this stuff up. Why, what's up?"

"*Top Chef* is about to come on."

"A'ight, let me go put this stuff up."

"Okay. Hurry up. It's really warm under here." Farrah lifted the blanket and revealed an all-black teddy.

"That's how you feel?" Mills smirked, feeling his dick become hard.

"Uh-huh." Farrah nodded, biting her bottom lip.

"You a nasty li'l girl." He grinned devilishly.

"You love it."

"You gon' bounce it?" Mills probed, playing with one of her nipples. He loved when he hit it from the back and Farrah made her ass jiggle.

"Only if you promise to hit me with the death stroke," she countered.

"I got you li'l lady. Let me go take a piss real quick and put this stuff up."

"How romantic." Farrah rolled her eyes.

Mills laughed and walked to the master bathroom and shut the door behind him. He'd never lied to Farrah before, and the confusing part of it all was he didn't know why he had. It was a simple question that deserved a simple answer. All he had to do was tell her the truth. It wasn't like he and Jade had slept together. The conversation on his part was innocent.

She'd done all of the confessing and it wasn't like he was planning on going back to her. Mills was good where he was at. So why was it he felt torn?

It was funny how a few words from Jade changed everything. Since he'd seen her Mills couldn't stop thinking about what she'd told him. He couldn't even hold a descent conversation with Farrah without flashbacks of Jade running through his head. *I miss you. I know I fucked up but I want you back,* replayed over and over in his mind. But why? He'd moved on. He was over her or so he thought.

Farrah was who he loved. She'd proven herself time and time again. As long as he remained loyal and respectful she'd always be there. A week had gone by since he went and picked up his things and ever since Mills found himself caught up in his thoughts. He often wondered if Farrah had noticed a change in him. She hadn't said anything so he figured she hadn't. As they lay snuggled up in bed, wrapped in each other's arms, watching *Unsung: Millie Jackson* a text message came through on Mills's phone. He swiftly turned over and grabbed his phone.

Farrah glanced at the clock. It was 12:30 a.m. She didn't say anything but she wondered who would be texting Mills that late at night. The insecure girl in her wanted to ask but the woman in her told her to chill and relax. She and Mills were straight. At first she was unsure. She thought that he would change his mind about them, but he'd done everything in his power to make her feel secure about their relationship and it worked. Farrah was at peace and comfortable with him. Although when she looked in his eyes lately she saw a glimpse of uncertainty. She'd tried her damnedest to ignore it but the longer she looked the more she became shaken.

Giving into temptation, Farrah glanced over her shoulder and asked, "Who is that?"

Mills finished replying to the message and turned off his phone. "My agent. We gotta meet up with the contractor for the skate park tomorrow."

"Oh." Farrah focused her attention back on the television.

As Mills retook her into his arms Farrah's heartbeat began to accelerate. She'd been here before. This was the moment where things in a relationship began to go downhill. Mills had just lied to her, and although she didn't know why she prayed it wasn't because of another female.

But the nervous tingling in her stomach told her it was. She knew this part of a relationship all to well to ignore the signs. Wanting desperately to give him the benefit of the doubt, Farrah kept quiet and made the mature decision to trust her man until he gave reason to do otherwise.

Chapter Eighteen

You know I gotta girl at home alone and if I keep fuckin' around wit' you she'll be gone.
—Trey Songz, "Girl At Home"

Diablitos Cantina, located in the heart of midtown St. Louis, was a hip, new Mexican street vendor-themed restaurant. Mills pulled up and immediately noticed the restaurant's quirky appeal. On the roof were two dinosaurs drinking tequila. Intrigued, Mills got out of the car and made his way inside.

For a second he stood in the entrance way and examined the crowd for Jade. He found her sitting at the bar with her legs crossed, sipping on a margarita. Once again he'd kept the truth from Farrah. There was no way he could tell her that he was even thinking about hearing Jade out, let alone meeting up with her. He didn't want to hurt or alarm her. They were just going to talk. He felt like he at least owed her that much.

"Hey." She waved, spotting him.

"How you doing?" He sat next to her on a stool.

"You look handsome." She took in his physique.

Although her feelings for him had wavered, Jade couldn't deny Mills's sex appeal. He'd donned a Chicago Bulls fitted cap cocked to the side, black T-shirt, a light denim jacket with a red handkerchief hanging out of the breast pocket, black fitted jeans, and Nike Air Jordans. Every chick in the spot was eying him but he was there with her, which made her feel good.

"Thanks. Ay," Mills said to the bartender. "Let me get a shot of tequila."

"So you ain't gon' tell me I look nice?" Jade frowned.

"That would be inappropriate." Mills cracked a smile.

"Oh, I forgot you got a girlfriend." Jade chuckled, rolling her eyes. "Who is this mystery girl by the way?"

"Does it matter? It ain't you," Mills shot.

"*Touché*." Jade smiled coyly. "I didn't ask you here to talk about your girlfriend anyway."

"Why did you?" Mills gulped down his shot before asking for another.

"Because I've been doing a lot of thinkin'—"

"You . . . thinkin' . . . nah," Mills joked.

"Whatever." Jade playfully pushed his arm. "Seriously, I think I'ma move."

"I've been meaning to talk to you about that." Mills drank his second shot. "That loft is too big for you and since we're not together no more I figured we'd sell it and split the profits."

"That's cool." Jade panicked. "But I was thinking much further than just moving into another place. I'm talking about moving to another state," she lied, hoping he'd take the bait.

"What you wanna do that for?"

"There's nothing here for me. We're not together. I don't have many friends and I've always wanted to get into modeling, so I figured I'd move to L.A. I've accepted the fact that we're through. I fucked up. I took you for granted and instead of telling you that I was unhappy I started to push you away."

"But that's what I don't get. Why were you unhappy?" Mills quizzed, dying to know.

"I don't know." Jade shrugged her shoulders. "I guess I just got bored. I wanted more."

"Didn't I try to give you everything you ever wanted?"

"Yeah, that's why I feel like such an ass. You were perfect. You're the best thing that's every happened to me." Jade gazed deep into his eyes.

"Let me ask you this, and tell the truth." Mills situated himself in his seat. "Were you seeing somebody else?"

"No," Jade replied with a straight face. "Can't nobody compare to you."

For a minute they sat in complete silence.

"Hey." Jade perked up. "Remember when you used to drive that Nissan Maxima and how it use to cut off on us all the time?" Jade laughed.

"Yeah." Mills cracked up laughing too. "I used to hate that shit but you stuck in there wit' me. You ain't even care."

"Those were the good ol' days."

"Yep," Mills agreed, taking another shot of Tequila.

"You going to see Idle Warship featuring Res and Talib Kweli? They gon' be at 2720 Cherokee," Jade said enthusiastically.

"I was thinking about going. Why?"

"You wanna go together?" Jade raised one of her brows.

"Uhhhhh." Mills hesitated. "That might be possible."

"Cool." Jade gleamed.

"So you sure about this whole moving thing?" Mills asked cautiously.

"I really think it's for the best. Unless . . . you got a reason for me to stay."

Mills fumbled around with his shot glass while he thought. He hadn't expected to come and actually enjoy Jade's company. This was the Jade he knew, loved, and honestly missed. Now he wondered if he had jumped to end things too quickly. Maybe he'd overreacted, but the feelings of disappointment, misuse, and hurt were all too real at the time. He couldn't deny or forget that. But here she was admitting her wrongs and trying to make amends. Up until recently they hadn't had any major problems. He suspected she was cheating but there was no physical proof of infidelity.

What the fuck, man? Mills turned his hat to the front. This shit was too much for him to handle. He loved two women and they both loved him. What was he to do: go back to the woman who'd held him down for six years, or stay with the woman who made his heart melt with a mere smile?

"Do you want me to stay?" Jade got up from her seat and stood between his legs. "Just say the word," she whispered, gripping the back of his head.

Mills's mind was screaming for him to tell her to back up but his limbs had gone limp. Jade's golden skin shined like the Sahara Desert. Her full lips were inches away from his. The sweet smell of her perfume was drawing him closer. The setting was right and the tequila shots had him feeling extra nice. Like magnets their lips pressed against one another. Kissing her was so wrong but somehow felt so right. Then, their tongues danced and the fireworks appeared.

"It's whatever you want," Jade said, coming up for air. "Just say the word and I'll stay."

Mills looked away. Regret swarmed him. He had no business being there with Jade. They'd been down this road before and she'd hurt him tremendously. She would probably do it again, yet there he sat, recklessly giving into doubt and temptation.

"Yeah," he finally answered. "Hold off on that for a minute."

Across town Farrah was leaving the St. Louis Galleria mall when she heard someone shout her name. Wondering who it was she looked over her shoulder and saw Khalil jogging toward her. *What the fuck does he want?* she thought, continuing to walk.

"Wait up!" Khalil shouted.

"What is it, Khalil?" Farrah reached her Jeep then spun around.

"How you been?" he asked, out of breath.

"Good." She frowned.

"You look good." Khalil licked his lips.

"Eww, don't be a creep." Farrah tuned up her face.

"I'm being real. You gettin' thick, girl." Khalil patted her on the thigh.

"Did you really stop me to have this conversation? If so I have somewhere to be." Farrah unlocked the driver-side door.

"Damn it's like that?" Khalil drew his head back.

"What other way would it be?" Farrah said with a sudden fierceness. "I ain't got shit for you, Khalil. You shouldn't even been talkin' to me unless you got some dollars in yo' hand for the months of unpaid rent you stuck me wit'."

"On my mama I got you," he promised.

"Yeah, just like you got every bitch in St. Louis."

"That was nothing. You know I only got feelings for you," Khalil said sincerely.

"I don't know shit so if you'll excuse me." She tried to get inside her car but Khalil stopped her.

"I miss you," Khalil confessed with a hint of desperation in his voice.

Farrah looked at Khalil with sorrow in her eyes. He was such a fool. She was so over him it wasn't funny. Months ago if he would've uttered those words to her it would've meant the world but now she couldn't give a damn. She now knew what real love felt like and his words were met with deaf ears. He finally realized what she'd known from the start, that the grass wasn't greener on the other side.

"I miss you too, Khalil, but I don't miss the drama and the lies. Have a good night." She hopped inside her Jeep and placed it in reverse.

Farrah was in complete shock and dismay. "That nigga must be crazy," she said out loud to herself. Being in Khalil's presence made her sick to her stomach. She couldn't stand the sight of him anymore. Love for him no longer existed. Being around him for that brief moment only made her appreciate Mills more.

An insurmountable amount of love for him filled her heart. Needing to hear his voice, she dialed his number and placed the call on speakerphone. Five rings later her call went to voice mail. Figuring he was still in his meeting, Farrah ended the call and continued home.

It was eleven p.m. when Mills returned home. His mind was so fucked up that he couldn't even think straight. Feelings he'd buried and burned for Jade had somehow risen like a phoenix and they'd wound up having sex in the restaurant's bathroom. If he could have, he would've blamed it on the alcohol, but he genuinely took pleasure in kicking it with her. Sex was never supposed to be part of the equation but the deed had been done and there was no taking it back. He'd fucked up so bad that he didn't even want to go home. Mills couldn't dare look Farrah in the eye without breaking down. She deserved better than what he was giving her.

As he placed his key into the lock his heart was so heavy he barely could breath. He felt even more like shit when he entered the house and found the lights dimmed low, candles lit, Miguel's mixtape hit "Arch n Point" playing, and Farrah sitting in a chair, naked, with three red bows strategically covering her nipples and pussy.

"What's all of this for?" Mills asked, surprised.

"This is my way of telling you how grateful and thankful I am to have you in my life." Farrah sauntered toward him slowly. "I know how hard you've been working on the skate park and I'm so proud of you." She took his jacket off.

Farrah swore she smelled the faint smell of a woman's perfume on him, but convinced herself that she was wrong.

"Thank you." Mills eyed her. He wasn't the type of a man to cry, but that night he felt himself on the verge of tears.

"Did your meeting go well?" Farrah draped her arms around his neck.

"It did." He held her close to his chest. "What you do today?"

"After work I went to the mall, that's it." She caressed his back and felt how tense he was. Farrah knew him like she knew the back of her hand; something was wrong. "What's wrong?" She hugged him tighter.

"Nothing, I'm good. Just tired, that's all." Mills rested his nose in the crook of her neck.

"Too tired to get you some of this?" She stepped back so he could get a good view of her frame.

"Please don't be mad, but I'm hella tired, babe. I just wanna go to bed. Is that all right?" Mills said, flushing in distress. He had too much respect for Farrah to fuck her and Jade in the same night.

"It's cool. I understand," she replied, visibly let down.

"You sure?"

"Yeah," Farrah said, feeling rattled. "I can't force you to have sex with me."

"It's not even about that. I love making love to you. I would just much rather chill out tonight."

"Okay." Farrah felt her face becoming hot.

"I'm gettin' ready to go take a shower." Mills gave her a quick peck on the cheek before heading to the bedroom.

Quietly Farrah blew out each of the candles as Mills turned on the shower. There was no denying it, or pretending not to notice the drastic change in him anymore. He was making it loud and clear that things between them had changed for the worse. The fact that he didn't want to have sex with her said it all.

There was someone else. For weeks she'd known it but the love she had for him begged her to turn the other cheek. The tears that filled every crevice of her face had other ideas. Mills was silently killing her. Like most women, Farrah wondered if she should pack it up and leave.

There was no point in waiting for his infidelity to hit her smack dab in the face. After dealing with Khalil she'd learned to trust her gut instinct. But if she left and found out she was wrong, then what? No, Farrah would swallow her fears and give Mills the benefit of the doubt.

Chapter Nineteen

When you left me, couldn't believe it. I thought that we had magic. I thought that we were special but it's over, huh?
— Jill Scott, "Quick"

Later on that week, Farrah sat watching the clock with sorrow in her eyes. It was 4:00 a.m. and Mills was out doing God knows what and with whom. She'd called him more times than she cared to count. The longer he didn't answer the phone and she sat smelling the leftover scent of his cologne in the air, the more she felt herself going insane.

How did I end up here again? She'd thought they had a mutual respect for another but apparently not. When he'd left he said he'd be home as soon as the club closed. All of the clubs in St. Louis had been shut down so the only place he could be was across the water in East St. Louis at a nightclub or strip club.

If not that, then he was in another woman's bed. Farrah prayed he was on the east side 'cause she couldn't stomach the notion of him being with another chick, but what honestly could it be? She'd experienced these types of nights with Khalil one too many times to not know the game. If a man wasn't answering his phone in the wee hours of the morning then he was doing nothing but creepin'.

Dialing his number once more Farrah held her breath and prayed to God that he would answer. Mills didn't though. Like all of the other times her calls went to voice mail. Pissed, Farrah tossed her cell phone down on the bed and folded her arms across her chest.

This was not how it was supposed to be. Mills was supposed to be different from Khalil and all of the other previous cats in her life. With each second that passed, breath she barely breathed, and thump of the heart, he, however, proved her wrong. As she sat idly by, pondering their outcome, Farrah felt the sensation of her phone vibrating. A sense of relief flooded over her as she rushed to answer.

"Hello?"

"What's up?" Mills said with a slight attitude.

"Where are you?" Farrah picked up on his attitude.

"On the east side."

Farrah could hear loud club music in the background. "Why haven't you been answering your phone?"

"'Cause I didn't hear it ring," Mills lied. He'd seen her call but didn't feel like being hit with a bunch of questions.

"So you didn't see me callin' you?" Farrah questioned, knowing he was lying.

"If I did I would've answered."

Farrah's body tensed up to the point she felt paralyzed. At first there was just a feeling of disconnect between them, but now Mills was making it clear that he didn't feel like being bothered with her.

"When are you coming home?" she asked, becoming angry.

"I'll be there in a minute," he answered dryly. Mills felt horrible for giving her grief but he couldn't help himself. The guilt he felt for fuckin' Jade was eating him alive, and like most men, when they fucked up, instead of admitting his betrayal Mills began to treat Farrah like she was the one with the problem. Like the uneasiness she was feeling was just a myth she'd created in her mind.

"What's really good, Mills? Do you not wanna fuck wit' me no more? If not just let me know," Farrah asked, fed up.

"Where is all of this coming from?" he groaned. "You mad 'cause I went out?"

"No, I'm mad 'cause you been actin' hella different lately. And I'm starting to feel like something is up."

"Man, ain't shit up. I just got a lot of shit on my mind but look . . . I'ma just talk to you when I get home."

Farrah really wanted to force the conversation, but the fear of hearing something she didn't honestly wanna hear put her on pause. "All right." She sighed, hanging up.

There in the silence of his bedroom Farrah stared at the wall. Tears fought to be released but Farrah didn't have the energy to become a weak mess. It was already hard enough to breathe. Each inhale of air was a struggle. *Why am I even here?*

This was the moment where Farrah had the chance to leave with her head held high and her dignity intact. She'd be the one in control of her fate. She didn't have to put herself through the torture of waiting around for the ball to drop. It was obvious that Mills was either cheating or had lost interest.

As much as Farrah wanted to leave, something within her heart still felt like she and Mills had a chance at something great. Instead of listening to her mind, Farrah went with her heart. Lying on her side, she pulled the covers up and waited for Mills to return home.

Words couldn't describe how torn up Mills was inside. For days he'd gone back and forth, picking over the pieces of his life, and he realized that the situation with Jade was breaking him down. No matter how hard he tried to push thoughts of her out of his brain his head wouldn't stop spinning.

The only thing that kept running through his mind was whether he should give her another chance or stay with Farrah. He'd grown to love Farrah so much. He was in love with her, but it was all so new. They'd moved pretty fast, so fast that he was now questioning it all.

Nothing with Farrah was a sure thing. They really didn't know each other. They were still in the "learning one another" stage, whereas he knew Jade inside and out. They'd had six years of endless conversations, laughter, fights, tears, and mind-blowing sex. He knew where things between them stood. In the last year they'd stumbled and gotten off track, but after spending time with her Mills was starting to think that maybe, just maybe, things between them could be okay. He didn't want to hurt Farrah because of his confusion, but what was he to do? He needed her like the sun needed the moon, but Jade's presence was undeniable as well.

All of the "should he's" or "shouldn't he's" were killing him. That's why, on a Wednesday night he and Teddy found themselves drinking at Bismark, formally known as Me'Shon's Bar & Grill. He needed something to ease his worries and Hennessy was just the thing to do it. The secret thoughts that consumed him had to be drowned out. Mills was on his third round and had no intention of slowing down.

"You going in, huh?" Teddy asked.

"I'm tryin' to get fucked up," Mills responded.

"A couple more of those and you will be."

"That's the plan." Mills took a shot of Hennessy to the head.

"What's on your mind?" Teddy asked, concerned.

"Dog . . ." Mills shook his head and sighed. "Jade tryin' to get back wit' me."

"Where that come from?" Teddy said, shocked.

"That's what I'm tryin' to figure out. She claim she was going through something."

"You believe her?"

"I ain't got no other choice. She was acting funny as hell but I never had any concrete proof that she was on some other shit. And . . ." Mills paused. "We had sex."

"Cuz, what is you doing?" Teddy grimaced.

"I know, I know," Mills agreed. "I already feel fucked up as it is."

"Farrah know?"

"Fuck naw . . . and you bet not tell London either."

"I ain't sayin' shit. That's y'all business," Teddy retorted. "What you gon' do?"

"I have no idea. I dig Farrah, I do. I love being wit' her. That's my baby. She means the world to me and I could see myself Spike Leeing her. You know, *Do the Right Thing,* ice cubes involved but . . ."

"Uh-oh—" Teddy chimed in.

"Nah, it ain't even like that. It's just . . . I don't' know what to do. I care about 'em both."

"Then the question is not who you can see yourself being wit', but who can you not see yourself being without?" Teddy gave him some words of wisdom.

Before Mills could even ponder the comment, Khalil patted him on the back.

"I ain't know y'all niggas was gon' be here," he remarked happily.

"What up, nigga?" Teddy spoke, shaking his hand.

"You can't speak, nigga?" Khalil said to Mills.

Not in the mood for pleasantries, Mills hit him with the infamous head nod.

"What y'all drinkin'?" Khalil asked.

"Hennessy," Mills replied.

"I'm good. Let me get a shot of Patrón," Khalil said to the bartender. "A nigga tryin' to get right tonight. As a matter fact a round is on me!" he shouted to the crowd.

"What's got you in such a good mood?" Teddy questioned.

"I'm finally gettin' my shit together. I won a race this past weekend and I ran into my baby the other day."

"Which chick is this?" Teddy remarked in a sarcastic tone.

"Farrah, who else?"

"Farrah?" Mills turned up his face. "When you see her?"

"Last Friday. She was coming out of the mall and we chopped it up for a minute. She told me she missed me and shit," Khalil boasted.

"Oh, word?" The veins in Mills's neck began to thump. "So she said she missed you, huh? That's cool." He licked his lips.

"You sure you ain't misunderstand her?" Teddy tried to defuse the situation.

"Nigga, I was there. I know what the fuck she said." Khalil looked at him funny.

"I just asked." Teddy looked at Mills out of the corner of his eye. He could see steam rise from his skin he was so pissed.

"I'm not feelin' too good. I'll check y'all some other time." Mills left a tip then got up and left.

"What's his issue?" Khalil took his seat.

"You heard the man. He ain't feeling well." Teddy gulped down the rest of his drink.

Mills's blood was boiling. The ride home was taking longer than normal. Maybe it was best, 'cause if Farrah was in front of him he would've killed her. She had him completely fooled. He just knew that she was this loving and devoted woman who would never do him wrong, but, no, she was a conniving, two-timing bitch. Here he was feeling like shit and she was playing him the whole time. Pissed, he stormed into his loft, shouting her name.

"Farrah!"

"Here I come," she yelled from the bathroom.

Once the toilet was flushed and she'd washed her hands, Farrah met up with him in the living room. A gigantic smile lit up her entire face.

"Baby, I got something to tell you." She beamed, jumping up and down.

"What? That you miss Khalil?" he replied indignantly.

"Huh?" Farrah said, caught off guard by his line of questioning.

"If you can huh you can hear!" He towered over her. "I ran into that nigga just a few minutes ago and he told me that he saw you at the mall Friday!"

"What are you talkin' about?" She stalled, becoming nervous.

"Farrah, straight up don't play wit' me." Mills closed his eyes and clasped his hands together. "Did you see him?" He opened his eyes.

"No," she lied, frightened.

"So you didn't see him?" Mills quizzed.

"I said no," Farrah huffed.

"So why he say he seen you then?"

"I don't know!" She shrugged, turning her back on him.

"Where yo' phone at? Call him then!" Mills snatched the pillows off the couch in search of her phone.

"I'm not doing all of that!" Farrah looked at him like he was insane.

"'Cause you lyin'!" Mills yelled. "Just tell the truth! You saw him didn't you?"

"Okay, I did!" Farrah finally admitted. "But I didn't say nothin' 'cause I knew you would spazz!"

"If it wasn't nothin' then what you lie for?" Mills raised his eyebrow. "'Cause it was something! 'Cause you was in that nigga face!" He pointed his finger at her like a gun.

"Pause! What is this really about? 'Cause this ain't even you right now! You doing a lot! You got something you need to tell me?" Farrah countered, folding her arms across her chest.

"Really, Farrah?" Mills said in disbelief. "Now you gon' try to switch this shit around on me! Nah, nah, nah." He paced back and forth. "It ain't even going down like that."

"Nah, answer the question!" Farrah mean mugged him. "'Cause you been actin' hella strange here lately!"

"Don't try and use that reverse psychology bullshit on me!" He stopped pacing and looked at her. "You the one lyin' and doing dirt! So what you was gon' do?" He stood in a boy stance. "Play me forever? What y'all gettin' back together? That's why he running around tellin' everybody you miss him and shit!"

"Miss him? What are you talkin' about? I didn't tell him that," Farrah replied defiantly.

"Then what did you tell him?"

"I . . . I . . . I told him . . ." Farrah stuttered.

"I . . . I . . . I . . . I . . . Cat yo' tongue, nigga?" Mills mocked her. "Did you say it?" Mills clapped his hands angrily. "Did you tell him that you missed him, Farrah?"

"Yeah, but—"

Mills cut her off. "Wow." He massaged his jaw and laughed.

"It's not what you think. Listen." Farrah took his hand into hers.

"Don't touch me." Mills shot her a look that could kill and yanked his hand away.

Farrah swallowed the huge lump in her throat and said, "All I said to him was that I missed him but that I didn't miss the drama. Khalil already knows that I'm wit' somebody else!"

"Really? How he know that?" Mills cocked his head to the side.

Fuck, Farrah thought. Now she'd have to confess to the conversation they'd had.

"You remember the night of my birthday when my phone rang? That was Khalil calling."

"So you mean to tell me you held a whole conversation with this man while I was asleep and that's supposed to make me feel better? I'm suppose to be cool wit' that! Have you gon' crazy?" he retorted, heated. "What you waiting on him to change so y'all can get back together? I guess I'm just the in-between nigga, huh? The rebound nigga!"

"No!" Farrah pleaded.

"That's why I ain't really invest that much in you!" Mills shook his head, appalled. "I don't even want that much from you! I just want you gone!"

"But I'm pregnant!" Farrah blurted out.

"Pregnant? How convenient!" Mills threw his hands up in the air, exasperated. "What is that some kind desperate ploy?" He screwed up his face. "That's the oldest, cheap-ass trick in the book! Yeah, okay, you pregnant! If you pregnant, I'm pregnant too," he shot in a sarcastic tone.

"Are you serious right now?" Farrah ignored his sarcasm.

"You think this is a game? I don't give a damn about you being pregnant! You better go look for the daddy!" Mills shouted hurt.

Farrah stared at him in shock, feeling as if she'd been back slapped.

"You pregnant!" Mills scoffed. "You are really something else! You know that? You are something else," he said with a laugh while wagging his index finger in her face.

"Will you stop carrying on and let me explain?" Farrah tried to reason.

"Nah, what for? You already lied twice! How you gon' explain a pregnancy? You gon' explain who the father is 'cause it ain't me!"

"What?" Farrah said, feeling her soul slip away. "Where is all of this coming from?"

"You need to ask yourself that. It's coming from you lying so deal wit' it," Mills said in an even tone.

"I can't believe you are even talkin' to me like this! You know me! I would never hurt you!" Farrah's voice cracked.

"I don't know you! I don't know you at all! As a matter of fact I don't even wanna get to know you! What I thought I knew about you was a lie! I just want you gone!"

"Are you serious?" Farrah said breathlessly.

"Yeah, dead serious." Mills took one last look at her then left as quickly as he came, slamming the door behind him.

Farrah waited for days for Mills to return home or return her calls, but he never did either. Each second that passed by she grew angrier and more hurt. She'd feared this happening. She'd feared that a day would come where he'd leave and she'd be left a weeping mess. After years of hiding how she really felt for him she finally opened up and he'd promised never to hurt her.

He'd seen the pain Khalil caused and here he was hurting her far worse than she could have ever imagined. Mills was supposed to be different. They were supposed to get married and raise their child together. But instead of living happily ever after, he was too busy accusing her of some foul shit she didn't even do. Instead of listening to her like he'd always done before, the first time some shit popped off he acted like an insecure asshole. This wasn't the man she knew, or had shared her deepest, darkest secrets with. This wasn't the man who'd promised to love her forever.

Someone she hated had taken him over and now she was left to her own devices. All that was left of her was a bag of bones. She couldn't find the strength to do anything. Even crying was a struggle. Farrah yearned for her sanity back because the longer Mills went without speaking to her she neared death. Tired of waiting for his return, Farrah mustered enough strength to gather her shell of a body and go home.

"Farrah, is that you?" London said from the top of the steps.

"Yeah." Farrah dragged her feet.

"I was starting to think you didn't live here anymore."

Farrah didn't even have the energy to respond. Getting from Mills's place to her own was hard enough. The morning sickness and heartache were wearing her body down and kicking her ass. She couldn't move another inch or part her lips to speak. The couch was calling her name. Farrah plopped down and rested her head on the back of the couch.

"What's wrong wit' you? You look like shit," London said from inside the kitchen.

Without warning the tears in Farrah's eyes that begged to fall dripped down her face and she began to weep.

"Farrah." London rushed to her side. "What's wrong?"

"I'm pregnant," Farrah wailed.

"Really?" London smiled. "Well that's a good thing, right?"

"No. Mills left me."

"What? Did you tell him you were pregnant?" London held her close.

"Yes."

"And he left you?" London yelled. "What kind of shit is that?"

"He thinks that I was cheating on him with Khalil but I wasn't. It was all a big misunderstanding but he won't listen to me. I don't know what to do. I just want all of this to go away," Farrah cried.

"It's gon' be okay, friend." London rocked her back and forth. "I promise. It's gon' be okay."

"No, it's not," Farrah cried into her chest.

"Listen." London pushed her back and held her at arm's length. "You have to pull yourself together. You have more than just you and Mills to think about now. You have a baby to attend to so stop all of this crying crap. If Mills don't wanna have nothing to do wit' you then fuck 'em. That's his loss. I'll be the baby daddy." She laughed.

"Shut up." Farrah giggled, wiping her eyes.

"Seriously, you know I got you. We can do this. We started a business together. Who says we can't raise a baby together."

"You would help me for real?" Farrah said somberly.

"Of course, you know I love you like a sister, or better yet a Birkin bag."

Chapter Twenty

I know your face, I know your name but I don't know you. Isn't that crazy?
—Jhene Aiko, "Stranger"

For two weeks Farrah did nothing but go to work, come home, and lie in bed. Her pregnancy and breakup were beating the shit outta her on a daily basis. She'd stopped trying to reach out to Mills. After her relationship with Khalil, she vowed that she would never allow herself to sweat a man under any circumstance. She loved Mills, she did, but she'd done nothing wrong. He was the one acting like an asshole and Farrah wasn't beat for trying to explain herself anymore.

She tried to talk things out. It wasn't her fault he didn't want to listen. She was done chasing men. She had other shit to worry about like her baby. From the looks of things she was going to be a single mother and she had to mentally prepare for that. It wasn't what she'd dreamt of or imagined, but these were the cards she'd been dealt. No matter how bad Mills treated her she was determined to handle herself with dignity and grace.

Fuck Mills! If he wanted to act a fool then he could do it by himself. And yes, each morning she woke up alone without him by her side was a struggle. All she wanted was to escape the misery she was experiencing but every day there it was staring her in the face. No matter how she tried to block it or run from it, pain followed her. She despised Mills for turning his back on her. Tears and anguish filled her veins every time she thought of him. She wished she could forget he even existed but the baby inside her wouldn't allow that to happen. Trying her damnest to be a big girl, Farrah took a client's measurements when a wave of tears poured from her eyes.

"Excuse me." She rushed out of the room and into the restroom.

"Farrah." London tapped lightly on the door.

"Just a minute." Farrah grabbed some tissue and blew her nose.

"Can I come in?"

"Yeah." Farrah wiped her nose.

"Are you okay, honey?" London came in and closed the door.

"Yeah, I just needed a break that's all." Farrah wiped her face.

"Farrah, it's okay to be sad." London rubbed her arm.

"No, it's not. I can't afford to be sad right now. We have a business to run—"

"And you have yourself and the baby to take care of," London added.

"I know it's just hard." Farrah exhaled, feeling defeated.

"Listen." London held both of her arms. "You and Mills need to talk 'cause this whole thing has gotten way out of hand. Tonight is the Idle Warship concert and Teddy told me he was supposed to be there so why don't you come?"

"No." Farrah shook her head. "Why should I try to talk to him again? I tried. He doesn't want to talk to me. I'm not running behind him no more. He should be running behind me."

"I agree but he's not 'cause he's upset and one of you has to be the bigger person for the sake of this baby."

Farrah rolled her eyes and stomped her foot. "I don't wanna be the bigger person. I'm tired of always being the bigger person," she pouted.

"Well, get over it, bitch." London patted her on the ass. "We're going and you two are gonna talk."

***

Mills was dead wrong and he knew it for not reaching out to Farrah, but he needed a minute to digest everything that had gone down. So much stuff was coming his way that he couldn't process it all. Jade was constantly in his ear telling him how much she loved him; Farrah possibly wanted to get back with Khalil and was possibly carrying his baby.

He knew deep down inside that the baby was his and he planned on being there for her, but he was in his feelings and couldn't get out of them. She'd lied to him not once but twice. He expected so much more from her and, honestly, himself. No other love compared to the one they shared, but the first chance he got he betrayed her in the worst way imaginable.

Mills was a victim of his own uncertainty. He'd let it take him over, and as a result his relationship with Farrah was in shambles. He'd cheated, she'd lied, and the trust they once held was gone. There were many minutes Mills found himself in the process of dialing her number, but silly pride stopped him each time. He missed his boo but maybe the drama swarming them was a sign.

Maybe they weren't meant to be. Mills still didn't know what he wanted. He could forgive her for lying, but would she be able to forgive him for sticking his dick in another woman? Mills fully intended on talking to Farrah. They had to work out their unresolved issues, but until then he just wanted to push all of his problems to the side and kick it.

The Idle Warship featuring Res and Talib Kweli concert was in full effect. Mills loved coming to see a show at 2720 Cherokee. It was an eclectic two-level venue that featured graffiti painting on the walls, vintage pinball machines, and an art gallery. As promised he attended the concert with Jade.

He'd made it clear that they would go together strictly as friends and she seemed to understand that, which was good. Being around her was a great distraction. Jade kept his mind off of Farrah, which was almost damn near impossible.

"Mmm, this Patrón margarita is delicious." Jade licked her lips, savoring the taste.

"It is fire," Mills agreed.

"You having fun?" She playfully hit him on the arm. "You seem distracted."

"I'm good," Mills lied.

"You sure? You know I know when you're upset," Jade persisted.

"I'm cool," Mills promised, unable to look her in the eyes.

"Okay." Jade shrugged, taking another sip of her drink.

Then DJ Needles began to spin Rihanna and Chris Brown's "Birthday Cake" remix, amping her up.

"Uh oh, this my shit." Jade snapped her fingers and swayed her hips to the beat. "Come dance wit' me." She took Mills by the hand and they began to two-step. "Remember how you did it? Remember how you fit it? If you still wanna kiss it, come get it," she sang to Mills while popping her ass.

Mills chuckled and watched her do her thang.

Unbeknownst to him, Farrah and London had just walked in. Farrah knew she'd see him there but never did she think she'd see him there with Jade, dancing, no less. Time instantly slowed and her heart rate declined. She couldn't feel her legs and her hands had gone numb. She wanted to fall to the floor and drown in a puddle of her own tears.

How could he humiliate me like this? She knew he was upset but she never thought he was so upset that he'd go back to Jade. Didn't he know that if she caught them together the mere sight would kill her? Better yet, did he even care? Then Farrah remembered the night he received the text message in the middle of the night and how his personality switched up afterward. *It was because of Jade,* she thought. *They were fuckin' around.*

"C'mon let's go." London tried to usher her back out the door.

"No." Farrah blinked back the tears that were begging to fall. "No." She walked over to Mills and stood in his face. "Really?" she said.

Mills immediately stopped dancing and stood frozen. For the past two weeks all he'd done was stare at pictures of her; now here she was, live in the flesh, looking like a beautiful nightmare.

"What's good?" Khalil approached them. "Damn you look good than muthafucka," he said to Farrah.

"Ya man talkin' to you." Mills glared at her.

"Fuck that. You're really here with her?" Farrah's bottom lip trembled. "After everything this is what you do? I'm pregnant, nigga!"

"You're pregnant?" Khalil repeated, shocked.

"She's pregnant?" Jade looked at Mills. "By you?"

"Yeah," Farrah responded for him.

"Y'all been fuckin'?" Khalil's lip curled. "You been fuckin' my girl? You supposed to be my boy!" He pushed Mills.

"Nigga, fuck you!" Mills pushed him back even harder.

"Stop!" Farrah yelled as people began to stare.

"I knew yo' ass wasn't shit! You fake-ass bitch! I should throw this fuckin' drink in your face!" Jade stepped up to Farrah.

"Bitch, I dare you! I will take these mutha-fuckin' heels off and go H.A.M. on everybody up in here! Now try me," Farrah warned.

"I can't believe you fucked this nigga. I should kill the both of y'all!" Khalil took off his jacket.

"You ain't gon' do nothing!" Farrah blocked his path.

"Nah, move, Farrah!" He tried to push her out of the way.

"No! Stop!" Farrah pushed him back.

"Let him by!" Mills charged toward them.

"Mills, stop!" Farrah placed her hand on his chest.

"Oh, so you gon' protect this man?" he shouted, outraged. "And you wonder why I think that's his baby!"

The first time he'd maliciously hurt her by uttering those words Farrah let it slide, 'cause she knew he was upset. But for him to say it again and in front of everyone was like him putting a gun up to her head and pulling the trigger.

"Fuck you!" She mushed him in the head. "I've had it! Fuck you and I mean it! Fuck you!" She shot daggers at him with her eyes, then stormed out.

"Farrah!" Mills followed her.

"Just leave her alone!" London tried to stop Mills.

"Stay out of this, London!" Mills rushed past her and ran outside after Farrah.

Rain was falling from the sky at a blinding speed. Mills was instantly drenched. "Farrah! Hold up!" He ran as rain pelted his face.

"Just go 'head, Mills!" Farrah speed-walked down the street. Her heels clicked loudly against the pavement. "I'm done! Be wit' the bitch! I don't care!" She flung her arm.

"But I do!" He caught up with her and held her by the waist from behind.

"Let me go, Mills!" Farrah tried to break loose but Mills's hold was too strong. "Just let me go!" she said more emotionally than figuratively.

"I can't!" Mills placed his wet face up against hers.

"I don't care! Let me go." Tears fell from her eyes.

"No!"

"Let me go!" She kicked him in the leg with the heel of her pump.

"Fuck!" Mills released her from his arms and massaged his leg.

"Stay the fuck away from me! I mean it!" Farrah's voice shook slightly.

Breathing heavily, she eyed him with sorrow in her eyes. Their relationship was done. They'd reached their climax and there was nowhere to go but down. Mills stood straight up and tried to inch toward her, but Farrah took two steps back. Mills would've given his left leg to hold her right then. The rain had caused her long hair to stick to her face and neck.

The skintight dress she wore clung to her skin, causing her hard nipples to show. At that moment the fear of losing her forever forced Mills to put everything into perspective.

Yes, she'd lied, but he'd done the unthinkable. If anybody deserved a second chance it was Farrah. He'd been a fool to allow his own foolish behavior to overshadow his love for her. He should've heard her out and been there for her. Now because of his selfish behavior it seemed like he'd lost the love of his life for good. Mills wasn't going to give up, though. What he and Farrah shared was too good to give up and he was willing to do anything to get it all back.

"Just let me talk to you." Mills tried to reach out for her again.

"No! Stay the fuck away from me," Farrah cried.

"You don't mean that."

"Yes, I do." She nodded.

"But I love you," Mills said, feeling her slip away.

"You love me?" Farrah said, taken aback.

Before Mills knew it Farrah had raised her hand and slapped the shit outta him.

"How dare you! You don't love me! You don't even know what love is! You don't give a fuck about me! I'm pregnant wit' yo' baby and you haven't picked up the phone and called me once! No, you're here at the Idle Warship concert kickin' wit' your ex-girlfriend! Like how much more disrespectful can you be? I thought Khalil was the worst, but you . . . you take the cake!" Farrah sobbed.

"Farrah." Mills stepped closer only for Farrah to step back again. "You act like you're the only one hurting! You hurt me too!" He pounded his fist against his chest. "This shit is fucked up! You told that man you missed him while you sat there the same night and confessed your love to me!"

"I tried to explain to you what happened but you were so caught up in your own shit that you wouldn't listen! Now you're here with her!" Farrah pointed toward the building. Her entire body was shaking. "I'm done! That was the last straw! Now stay the fuck away from me!" she spat, getting into her car.

Mills stood on the sidewalk helplessly and watched as Farrah pulled off. As soon as her car turned the corner he felt his soul leave his body. She was his sun, his moon, his earth, but now he'd lost her. She was a good girl. She made a nigga feel good. All she wanted was to feel secure. How could he have fucked things up so bad? He was a better man than what he was presenting.

"You could've told me you were seeing her," Jade said from behind.

"Not now, Jade."

"Then when? Let's not forget you fucked me a couple of weeks ago," she spat with an attitude.

"Let's get something straight." Mills glared at her. "I ain't have to tell you shit. Me and you aren't together."

"So you weren't seeing her the whole time we were together?" Jade gave him a mock-glare.

"No."

"Like I'm really supposed to believe that. All that time you were accusing me of cheating you were the one doing dirt." She rolled her neck.

"Believe what you wanna believe. I honestly don't give a fuck." Mills walked away.

"Go ahead! Walk away like you always do! The shit must be true!" Jade yelled.

Mills didn't even have the energy in him to fight. The worst thing in life that could've happened had occurred. His baby was gone and it was his entire fault. Mills didn't know how he'd go on without her. Regret filled his limbs. He already couldn't function. Something had to be done. He just didn't know what.

Chapter Twenty-one

An angel in disguise she was but still somehow you fell for her.
—Brandy, "Angel in Disguise"

"Girl, you will not believe what happened at the concert the other night," Jade said to Deion over drinks. Both women sat in their designer frocks sipping on cosmopolitans.

"What?" Deion said, dying to know.

"Girl . . . you know that broad Farrah I was tellin' you about?" Jade popped her lips.

"Yeah." Deion nodded eagerly.

"Well guess what? The bitch is pregnant." Jade pursed her lips together.

"And?" Deion screwed up her face. "What that got to do wit' you?"

"By Mills, bitch," Jade stated.

"Get the fuck outta here!" Deion almost dropped her glass.

"Yes, so apparently they've been messing around." Jade rolled her eyes.

"I told you not to sleep on her." Deion covered her mouth and giggled.

"Oh whatever." Jade waved her off.

"Don't 'whatever' me 'cause she got yo' man."

"She ain't got shit 'cause he was at the concert wit' me," Jade sneered.

"You are a mess." Deion shook her head. "So hold up. You still haven't talked to Rock?"

"Nope." Jade crossed her legs. "He hasn't called me and I haven't called him. I love him but I ain't gon' sweat no nigga. I'm too fly for that shit."

"You got that right." Deion tapped her glass against hers. "So how do you feel about Farrah being pregnant?"

"I'm hurt a li'l bit, I guess," Jade replied simply.

"A li'l bit? Bitch, I would be on the floor crying. Do you even have a heart?" Deion said, stunned.

"Of course I do. It bothers me that she's pregnant but hey what can I do? Now what would've killed me if it were Mya who was pregnant by Rock. Now that shit would've rocked my world."

"So you really don't feel anything for Mills anymore? You just using him at this point?"

"Pretty much. I can't be without a man. What am I going to do get a job? Uh, no." Jade rolled her neck. "Somebody gotta take care of me."

"How about you take care of yourself?" Deion opposed her.

"I'm not like you. I don't have any goals or ambition. My entire life I've been taken care, first by my parents then Mills. I've become accustomed to this life and I ain't tryin' to give it up."

"Just remember you reap what you sow," Deion warned.

"Ugh whatever, Debbie Downer aka Jennifer!" Jade referred to Jennifer from *Basketball Wives.* "You just mad 'cause I got two Chads and you don't have nothing," she joked.

"Bitch, you ain't gotta bring my breakup into the equation."

"You know I'm just playin'." Jade tapped her on the hand. "We gon' find you a new boo and me one too."

"You are the absolute worst." Deion giggled.

"I'm tryin' to get it how I live, boo boo." Jade popped her lips as her cell phone rang. "Mmm." She curled up her lip.

"Who is that?" Deion tried to look at the screen.

"Hello?" Jade answered instead of responding to Deion.

"Hey," Rock spoke.

"Hey," Jade replied softly.

"You busy?"

"Kind of. Why? What's up?" she said, feeling her entire body begin to shake.

"I was just callin' to see what was up wit' you. You've been on my mind so . . ."

"I've been on your mind, huh?" Jade repeated. "I couldn't have been on your mind too much. You haven't called me in I don't know how long."

"Yeah 'cause the last time we talked you went off on me so I figured I'd give you a minute to get yourself together."

"You can't be serious." Jade shook her head disbelievingly.

"I'm not but the last time we talked things were pretty fucked up," Rock said cautiously.

"Where is Mya?"

"I don't know. I haven't talked to her."

"What happened to y'all tryin' to work things out?" Jade shot mockingly.

"It didn't work. We realized that it was a bad idea. But look I ain't call you to get off into all of that. I called you to tell you that I fucked up and I miss you."

"You sure did," Jade said, relishing the fact that the ball was back in her court.

"I did and I'm sorry. I got some free time so I wanted to see if I could come see you."

"I don't know, Rock. The last time we saw each other it didn't go to well and you really hurt me." Jade continued to play the victim.

"Let me come see you then so I can make it up to you."

Jade didn't want to give in so quickly, but she missed Rock too much to play games. "A'ight, when you wanna come?"

"Is this weekend cool?" he questioned.

"Yeah." She jumped for joy on the inside.

"I'll call you later then."

"Okay." Jade ended the call.

"You a damn fool." Deion frowned.

"What?" Jade responded blankly.

"That nigga strung you along for an entire weekend then dropped yo' ass over the phone instead of to your face and you gon' let him come back that easy. Shiiiiiit," Deion said like an old woman. "Ain't no way."

"You don't understand. I love him."

"But he don't love you," Deion reminded her.

"You don't know that. If he didn't feel some kind of way about me he wouldn't keep coming back."

"He keep coming back 'cause he done found him a dummy." Deion laughed.

***

Ever since the concert Mills had been blowing up Farrah's phone nonstop. He'd sent text after text apologizing but she wasn't feeling him at all. He'd done the unthinkable and she just wasn't willing to forgive him and forget. Nothing he had to say mattered, because the love she thought they shared was tainted.

Plus, she couldn't get over how he'd hurt her. As much as she wanted to trust him and try again the damage was done. He'd left her for dead when she needed him most. All of the "I'm sorry's" in the world couldn't take away the sadness he'd caused. Farrah felt betrayed, like he'd spit in her face.

And so what that he was sorry? He wasn't sorry when he broke up with her, or when she told him she was pregnant and he accused her of lying. He wasn't sorry when he put her out of his house and neglected to call her for days. Mills was nothing but a sorry muthafucka.

But Farrah only had herself to blame. When she met him he belonged to someone else and when they'd lain down and made love he still did. Farrah should've never made herself believe that he'd get over a six-year relationship so quickly. His feelings for Jade would always trump the ones he had for her.

Farrah was nothing but a rebound. She was tired of competing for his affection. Jade could have him. She didn't want to be someone's second choice. If she wasn't his first choice, his one and only, then she would be nothing.

"Farrah, you have a call on line one," Camden said from her desk.

"Who is it?" Farrah flipped through Alice + Olivia's spring 2013 lookbook.

"Mills."

"Tell him I'm not here," Farrah replied dryly.

"You sure?" Camden asked, wishing they'd talk. "He's been callin' you for a week now."

"Yes!" Farrah slammed down the book. "Now will you all quit asking me that! I have nothing to say to him!"

"But he's your baby daddy. You're gonna have to talk to him sooner or later," London chimed in.

"No, I won't," Farrah disagreed.

"And how is that possible?" London quizzed, placing her hand on her hip.

Farrah paused. She'd been doing a lot of thinking and she realized that her heart couldn't take any more disappointments. She wanted one day to have a baby but now wasn't the right time. Her career was taking off and things with Mills in her mind were over. Things were already complicated and a baby would only complicate things more. No, Farrah would do herself and everyone involved a huge favor.

"'Cause I'm gonna have an abortion that's how." Farrah got up from her seat.

"No, you're not." London's jaw dropped.

"Yes, I am. What I look like keeping this baby and he's back with that dizzy broad? No. I'm gonna have an abortion and keep it moving." Farrah tried to sound sure of her decision.

Chapter Twenty-two

**I'm sick and tired of these hoes, playin'
that role on the low, claiming they
faithful and shit.
—Ace Hood feat. 2 Chainz, "Luv Her"**

Anxiously, Jade stood in the mirror applying a thin coat of M·A·C Pink Poodle lip gloss. All week she'd been preparing for Rock's arrival but nothing she did calmed her down. Nervous energy filled every inch of her frame. She couldn't wait to see his face and to be able to look him in the eyes. It'd been too long since they last saw one another.

She prayed they'd never go this long again. This time had been hard enough. Thankfully everything was working in her favor. Now that Rock had come to his senses she didn't have to deal with Mills anymore. Being around him was fun. It reminded her of when they first met, but unlike when they first met the eternal flame that once drew her to him no longer was lit.

Mills had become more of a friend with benefits, a pot'nah so to speak. With Farrah being pregnant there was no way they could be together. Jade was too fly, too pretty, too vivacious, and too into herself to be helping raise somebody else's baby. Besides, if she was gonna play Mama to anybody's baby it would be her own.

Now that her baby Rock was back in the picture where he belonged hopefully, just hopefully, he'd be open to one day building a family of their own. Jade wasn't willing to give up on her dream. It was more tangible than ever. The fact that Rock had time to think about what and who he wanted and he chose her showed that a piece of her held court in his heart.

During their separation her heart was broken and Deion was right. She shouldn't have forgiven him just after one phone call. But who wanted to deal with heartache? Deion wasn't the one who had to deal with trying to convince herself not to miss him. She wasn't the one who couldn't do anything but pray to God each day that he'd miss her enough to call.

She most certainly wasn't the one who had to deal with the nauseating pang in the center of her chest. Why go through that when she could forgive him and erase all of the pain and agony away? Jade examined herself in the full-length mirror from side to side. Her blond buzz cut was freshly bleached and trimmed. The black jersey spaghetti-strap maxi dress she wore clung to her breasts, hips, and thighs.

Jade looked so good that she turned herself on. Then the doorbell rang and the butterflies in her stomach took flight. *Here we go,* she thought, jogging down the steps. Trying to create a sexy mood, Jade quickly turned on the fireplace and pushed the volume up on the stereo.

"Okay," she exhaled, opening the door.

Right away Rock's eyes scanned her face and voluptuous frame. "Where you going?" he asked.

"Nowhere," she replied nervously.

"You sure? 'Cause that dress is the truth, Blondie."

"Come in." She opened the door wider.

Rock walked slowly inside and turned around to get a good view of her ass as she closed the door.

"Where are your bags?" Jade caught him ogling her.

"At the hotel. I didn't know if it was okay for me to bring 'em here."

"Oh," Jade said, slightly let down. Now that he was there, she didn't want Rock to have to leave for any reason at all. "Where you staying at?"

"The Four Seasons."

"Have a seat." Jade sat down on the couch.

Rock peeped the sexy vibe she had going on and got more comfortable by taking off his jacket. "What you been up to?" he asked, sitting next to her.

"Nothing much." Jade played coy.

"Uh-huh," Rock said, knowing she wasn't being all the way honest. "You look good." He eyed her hungrily.

"I know I do," Jade remarked, knowing she was the shit.

"You still got that smart-ass mouth I see."

"Ain't nothing changed. I mean except for you of course," she teased.

"So we at that part of the conversation, huh?" Rock smiled uncomfortably.

"Yep, you hurt me."

"That wasn't my intention though. I was just trying to figure things out and I didn't wanna hurt you in the process. But you just kept on pushing and pushing."

"So this is my fault?" Jade's face grew hot.

"I didn't say that. What I'm sayin' is Mya is my son's mother—"

Jade rolled her eyes and said, "Do we have to talk about her?"

"Stop actin' like that and listen." Rock took her hand in his. "We thought we should give it another try for TJ's sake. But right off the bat we knew it wasn't going to work and I couldn't stop thinking about you. Not being around you and not talking to you bothered me more than I honestly thought it would."

"Well, that makes me feel great," Jade scoffed.

"I'm just sayin'. I knew I that cared for you but I didn't know that I loved you."

Jade couldn't help but smile. *Hot damn! He finally said it*, she screamed inside.

"Say that again."

"You heard me, man. I love you." He pulled her close.

"I love you, too." Jade straddled him. She was more in love with him than ever.

"How much?" Rock palmed her ass cheeks.

"This much." Jade unbuckled his belt and unzipped his jeans. Seconds later his dick was out. Just the sight of his dick made Jade wet. Turned on to the fullest she lifted her dress and eased down onto his dick. Passionately she kissed his lips.

"Aww yeah! Yeah! Ooooooh yeah!" She bounced up and down.

"Ride that dick!" Rock slapped her on the ass, making her go faster.

"Ahhhhhhhhh," Jade screamed. "Awwwww fuck! This dick is so fuckin' good!"

Rock cupped each of her breasts in his hand and pounded her pussy with no remorse.

"Fuck! I'm gonna cum!" Jade held on to him tight.

"Me too," Rock groaned, cumming inside of her.

After cumming herself Jade found herself wanting more. "I gotta taste it." She slid down onto her knees and took him into her warm mouth. Rock's dick tasted like wine. The more she licked and sucked the drunker she became.

"Ahh!" She moaned, coming up from air.

"Damn." Rock eyed her with an intense look of desire.

"You want me to stop?" Jade taunted him by lightly licking the tip repeatedly.

"No." Rock closed his eyes, relishing the sensation.

"I didn't think so." She put his entire dick in her mouth.

Superhead didn't have shit on Jade. She could suck the skin off a dick. Jade was so into sucking his dick that she didn't even hear the sound of Mills putting his key into the door. After the debacle at the concert they hadn't talked. That night was such a mess and so many people's feelings were hurt that Mills didn't want to cause anyone any unnecessary pain, so he laid low.

Enough time had passed though. It was time for him to let Jade know exactly where things between them stood. He'd finally given Teddy's statement some thought. Surprisingly it didn't take long to come to the conclusion that he could live with Jade for another six years if he chose to. They'd go on unfulfilled, wishing they'd gone after true love instead of settling. But that's wasn't the life Mills wanted.

That life would be miserable and even if he put his all into it there was no way he could live without Farrah. It would be like trying to break an addiction. He couldn't do it. She was his rib and the woman God put him on earth to be with. He just prayed that he hadn't hurt her so bad that she'd never want to see him again.

But first he had to deal with Jade. Mills pushed open the door and was shocked to find Jade on her knees going H.A.M. on NBA superstar Tyrin Rhodes's dick.

"What the fuck?" Mills slammed the door so hard the walls shook.

"Mills!" Jade jumped, causing spit to fling from her mouth. "What are you doing here?" She shot up from the floor.

"What the fuck you mean what am I doing here? This is my fuckin" house!" Mills barked, ready to kill.

"Since when?" Jade cocked her head back.

"Since I been paying bills up in this mutha-fucka," Mills shot back.

"Oh, excuse me," Jade said sarcastically. "My fault, I'm sorry." She blinked her eyes. "I thought you moved out. I thought you moved in wit' another bitch!"

"Let me get the fuck outta here." Rock zipped up his jeans and picked up his jacket.

"No, wait!" Jade reached out for him.

"Get the fuck off me!" He snatched his arm away.

"Let me explain," she panicked.

"I don't wanna hear shit!" Rock shot her warning glance. "Yo." He turned and looked at Mills. "My fault. I didn't know."

Instead of responding, Mills simply hit him with a look that said, "nigga, please," as he walked out of the door.

"Rock!" Jade screamed, feeling like she was about to flip. "Come back," she begged from the door.

"You might as well run after him but when you do make sure to take all of your shit wit' you! Fuckin' dirty bitch!" Mills fumed. "You ain't shit!"

Jade slowly turned and faced him.

"I'm not shit?" She put her hand up to her chest in disbelief. "I'm not shit and you been playin' house wit' a whole other bitch!" She pointed her finger at him. "What you thought I was gon' lie here and wait for you? I don't love you! I been fuckin' him," she stressed, fuming. "And it wasn't the first time and it for damn sure won't be the last, 'cause it's good." She spat in Mills's face. "And I love him and I want him!"

"I don't give a fuck what you do. You ain't gon' be fuckin' him in my house," Mills said firmly. "I pay the bills up in here not you."

"You's a dumb muthafucka you know that!" Jade laughed in his face. "Didn't nobody tell you to continue to pay bills over here! You did it 'cause you wanted to! You was payin' bills over here 'cause you thought I was some dumb bitch you could just run back to when you got tired of that silly bitch!" She pointed her finger forcefully. "Well guess what? You came back and you got what your hand was called for! Don't be mad! 'Cause I'm fuckin' glad! I'm glad you found out! Now I don't have to deal wit' yo' tired-ass no more," Jade said with so much venom it sent chills up Mills's spine."Why are you even over here?" She looked him up and down like he wasn't shit. "Farrah must've left you! She must've found out that you were as wack as I knew you were!"

"You done?" Mills said, unfazed. "'Cause all that you doing ain't doing nothing but slowing you up from gettin' your shit. I was gon' be nice to you and give you a week but after all that shit now you got an hour."

"Nigga, please, I ain't going nowhere. My name on the lease too." Jade pursed her lips and rolled her neck like a ghetto girl. "Now what you gon' do?" she challenged.

"I'ma take you"—Mills towered over her—"and all of yo' shit and toss you out the muthafuckin' door. Now try me," he challenged. "'Cause you two seconds from gettin' fucked up already."

"You gon' have to put me the fuck out then . . . 'cause I'm not leaving," Jade said unwaveringly. "Now if you'll excuse me. I'm about to take a shower." She left him standing there.

After showering and changing her clothes Jade returned to the living room to find Mills still there. Never one to back down from a fight she took her rightful place on the couch and crossed her arms. She would be damned if he thought he was going to run her up out of her own house.

Mills sucked his teeth. The Chris Brown in him wanted to leap across the room and beat the shit out of her, but Mills wasn't that kind of dude. Putting your hands on a woman was for suckas. Nah, Mills wouldn't put his hands on her. He would beat Jade at her own game.

For three hours they sat in silence, shooting each other dirty looks. Neither was willing to budge. One of them was going to have to go. Mills watched as Jade sat tapping her foot. He could tell that she didn't want to be there. He didn't want to be there either. He would've much rather been with Farrah. But here they were tied up in a silly war.

Whether he left or she did neither of them was going to win in the end. A relationship that once meant the world had come to an end. Instead of fighting to hold on to something that had vanished eons ego, Mills decided to let bygones be bygones. He wasn't in love with her and she for damn sure wasn't in love with him. It was time for them to say good-bye.

"Listen—" He sat up.

"Go ahead wit' that bullshit, Mills, 'cause I'm not leaving." Jade rocked back and forth.

"I'm not even on that no more." He waved her off. "This shit that we doing is dumb. It's obvious that you've moved on and so have I."

Jade glared at him out of the corner of her eye.

"Ain't no need in tryin'a hold each other up. What we had has run its course. It was good while it lasted but I don't wanna fight wit' you no more. I just wanna be at peace wit' you so that means that I gotta say peace to you."

Jade stopped rocking and sat quiet. "I'm sorry," she said at once. "I shouldn't have had him in here."

"I don't even give a fuck. It is what it is." Mills sighed, standing up.

"What are we gon' do about the house?" Jade looked up at him.

"It's yours now. You can have it. I'll sign everything over to you," Mills said regrettably.

He hated that things between them were ending on such a sore note. He never thought they'd end up here.

Jade watched as Mills eased out the door. A part of her felt as if a piece of her was leaving with him. They'd grown up together and at one point were best friends. It would be weird not having him in her life anymore, but in life some things had to come to an end.

Chapter Twenty-three

Everybody has an addiction, mine happens to be you.
—Drake feat. Lil Wayne and André 3000, "The Real Her"

Once Mills was gone Jade didn't waste any time calling Rock, but as she anticipated he wouldn't pick up the phone. Not willing to accept defeat Jade grabbed her keys and drove to the Four Seasons hotel. She had to catch him before he decided to leave, if he hadn't already. Every single moment that passed and she wasn't near him felt like an eternity.

She had to get him. She had to talk to him so she could make things right. At the hotel Jade double-parked her car and got out. Tears instantly formed in her eyes. Rock stood on the sidewalk as the doorman placed his bags into the trunk of his car. If she'd arrived a second later she would've missed him.

"Rock!" she called out frantically. "Wait!" People outside turned and looked like she was a lunatic but she didn't care.

Rock glanced in her direction and rolled his eyes. Jade was wasting her time. He didn't have anything to say her.

"Rock." Jade rushed toward him. "You have to let me explain."

"Explain what, that you more foul than a muthafucka?" He grimaced. "And you wonder why it took me so long to open up to you. I knew you wasn't shit when I started fuckin' wit' you, but I tried to give you the benefit of the doubt. Shame on me." Rock shook his head.

"It wasn't even like that. We're not together," Jade tried to clarify.

"But y'all were together all those times you had me in that nigga crib! You don't do no shit like that! Niggas have died over shit like that!"

"I know what I did was wrong but I just wanted to be wit' you," Jade said desperately.

"Well now you've lost me," Rock said firmly.

"But you love me remember."

"I'm done, Jade. I already went through enough bullshit wit' Mya. I'm not about to do it wit' you." He opened the driver-side door.

"Let me just talk to you," Jade begged, feeling sick.

"Nothin' else needs to be said, I'm done." Rock got in and locked the door.

A million tears ran down Jade's face as she watched Rock pull off. She wanted to curl up on the ground in the fetal position. The fighter in her wasn't prepared to give up but nothing she said was going to help. She'd done the worst thing she could, which was hurt him. Only time apart and the willingness to forgive could heal that.

But what was she to do when he had her heart hemmed up in the palm of his hand? Being with Rock was as necessary as the air she breathed. Accepting defeat, Jade returned to her car. Inside she rested her folded arms on the steering wheel. The tears that poured from her soul wouldn't stop. It was like her soul was on emotional overload. Jade didn't know if she would be able to cope. The man she adored was gone and it didn't matter if she begged or if she cried, Rock would never deal with her again.

All Farrah could do was hold on to the white sheet and look up at the sterile ceiling above. A thin hospital gown covered her body as she lay on a hospital bed with her feet in stirrups. What she was doing was going against everything she stood for but she had no choice. She couldn't possibly have a child with Mills now that he was back with Jade.

She couldn't even bear talking to him. How would she be able to raise a child with him? It would kill her if she had to constantly see him with someone else, especially when it was her he was meant to be with. It had to be done. There was no way around it. She'd played herself once by thinking he actually loved her. She wouldn't play herself again by having his baby. Life was hard enough. She wouldn't dare bring a baby into their madness.

"Farrah," a nurse said sweetly.

"Yes." Farrah tried to blink back the tears in her eyes.

"You're gonna feel a little pinch." The nurse stuck a needle into her arm.

As the anesthesia flowed through her veins Farrah reluctantly eased her hand down her chest to her stomach. She was only a little bit over two months pregnant. Ever since she was a little girl she'd seen herself as a mom. The decision she was making would undoubtedly haunt her forever.

There was no turning back now. The anesthesia was taking over and her eyes were getting heavy. As her eyes closed and Farrah faded into dreamland the only thing she could picture was Mills's face.

Mills had had enough. He was over Farrah ignoring him so he decided to take matters into his own hands and hit her with an unexpected visit at her job. It was time for them to put all of the bullshit aside and work things out. He was done with her shutting him out. Yes, he deserved for her to give him her ass to kiss but enough was enough. They had to put their differences aside if for nothing more than the baby.

Mills, however, didn't want to just co-parent. He wanted them to become one again because together they were magnificent. On top of that he couldn't go another day without her. The nights he spent alone were pure torture. To not have her there by his side to be able to inhale her intoxicating scent was the equivalent of dying a slow death. His house was no longer a home. There was no way he was going home without her.

Anxiously anticipating seeing her adorable face, Mills walked into her office.

Camden, who was at her desk, noticed him immediately. "Hi." Her eyes popped out of their sockets she was so stunned to see him.

"How you doing? Is Farrah here?" Mills surveyed the room for her.

"No," London answered instead.

"You know where she's at?" Mills faced her.

"I sure do," London responded with an attitude.

"Look I know you ain't feelin' me right now but if you could please tell me where she's at I'd appreciate it. I really have to speak to her."

"Let me say this to you. What you did to Farrah was foul, so foul that she still hasn't recovered. So, if you know you're only going to hurt her again then, please, do her a favor and leave her alone. She can't take anymore shit from you. She's gone through enough."

"I'm not here to hurt her. I'm tryin' to make things right but I can't if I don't know where she's at."

London was about to go against the girl code, but in order for her friend to gain any kind of closure it was a must that she snitch. "She's at home."

"Bet," Mills said, pleased.

"Here." London went inside her purse and handed him her house key.

"What's this for?" he asked, confused.

"She's not feeling well so you'll have to let yourself in."

"Is she cool? Is the baby a'ight?" Mills asked, worried.

"I'll let her tell you that."

Farrah lay in bed with her pajamas on. She was bleeding heavily and her pelvis was still sore. But what caused her the most pain was the reality of what she'd done. More than anything she wished she could drink her pain away. Depression had set in and all she could was cry.

Her baby was gone and more than ever she wished it were back inside her womb. She'd childishly allowed her emotions toward Mills to cloud her better judgment and now she was suffering the consequences. All day long she'd done nothing but toss and turn, turn and toss. Farrah would give her right hand to rewind time and take everything back.

Then maybe her dream of her and Mills living in a big house with a white picket fence and them driving a four-door car with a car seat in the rear could come true. But none of that would ever come to fruition. It was all over now and a mere memory. She'd have to live with the choice she made whether she liked it or not.

"I just want a drink," Farrah exclaimed, kicking the cover off of her. "I just wanna get out of here," she groaned.

But in her condition she wasn't going anywhere. She was stuck, confined to her bed and the gloom she so wanted to run from. For the first time life was giving her a big F.U. and making her face her demons. All of her life Farrah wanted to experience the fairytale romance she'd read about in books. She'd assumed that if she loved a man wholeheartedly and provided him with his every desire she'd get the same in return, and maybe that was true for some. But Farrah continuously gave herself to men who were emotionally unavailable. When she met Khalil he didn't want a relationship but she pursued him anyway. All of the warning signs were there but she turned her cheek to them all.

Despite his downfalls Mills was a good guy overall, but she should've allowed him the time he needed to heal from his and Jade's relationship before they got together. Maybe then they would've stood a fighting chance because then he would've had a clear idea of what he wanted.

Hell, she still hadn't fully healed from her and Khalil's tumultuous relationship. Farrah saw a vision of love in Mills's eyes and fell hook, line, and sinker. She didn't give herself time to think about it, or ponder the repercussions. She wanted Mills and she got every bit that came along with him, from the uncertainty to the drama and the lies.

Then through the darkness that had swarmed her came a hint of light. Farrah couldn't believe her eyes. Mills had suddenly appeared from nowhere. She was so caught up in her thoughts that she hadn't heard him come in.

"Hi."

"How did you get in here?"

"London gave me her key."

"When did you see London?"

"I went up to your office."

"Well, I don't know what she did that for. You can leave." Farrah turned her back to him.

"I know you're mad and you have every right to be but will you just hear me out? We can't continue to go on like this."

"We don't have anything to talk about. There's nothing keeping us together so you have no reason to be here."

"What's that supposed to mean? Please don't tell me you went and did something stupid" Mills's heart rate increased rapidly.

Farrah didn't respond. She focused all of her attention on the wall and prayed to God that Mills would get the hint and leave, 'cause if he stayed a minute longer she was sure to burst into tears.

"Farrah!" he called out her name. "Look at me." Mills climbed into bed with her and forced her to face him. "Did you have an abortion?"

Farrah could see the fear in his eyes. She hated to crush his spirits, but he was going to find the truth out sooner or later.

"Yes." She diverted her attention elsewhere.

"Why would you do that?" Mills's voice rose slightly. "I was gon' come back. I just needed a minute to get my mind right. I told you I would never leave you."

"But you did." A tear trickled down Farrah's face. "Everything that you said you wouldn't do you did. You left me! What was I supposed to do?"

"I tried to talk to you but you wouldn't hear me out."

"I was mad."

"So mad that you had to get an abortion?"

"You left me and went back to Jade!" Farrah hit him in the chest. "What the fuck was I supposed to do? You wouldn't talk to me!" She hit him again.

"I'm not back with Jade!" He grabbed her wrist and shook her. "I never was! I just went to the concert wit' her that's all. Didn't shit pop off between us." He lied so easily.

"How am I supposed to believe that?"

"'Cause I'm tellin' you. Did Jade try to get back wit' me, yes. Was that part of the reason I started acting differently, yes. I'm not gon' lie, I was fucked up there for a second. But it didn't take me long to realize that what me and Jade had was dead. I love you.

"And I know I hurt you. I gotta live wit' that shit every day. It fucks me up to know that you're sad because of me. I never wanted you to feel like I didn't love you 'cause I do. And honestly I can't even get mad about what you did 'cause I'm the one who put you in a fucked-up position. Instead of talking to you I shut down, which I have to learn not to do. I just want you back, babe. I swear to God on everything I love that I will never do anything to hurt you ever again."

"So is this the part where I'm supposed say that all is forgiven 'cause it's not. Fuck you! You sorry." Farrah looked at him like he was dumb. "Well, guess what? I'm sorry too! I'm sorry that I ever fucked wit' you!"

"So you're not willing to give us another chance?"

"What part don't you understand? I'm done. There is nothing left between us."

"You don't love me?"

"That's not the muthafuckin' point! I loved you and you still left! Now, get out."

"Babe . . ." He tried to hug her.

"No!" She pushed him off of her, even though every inch of her skin wanted to feel him. "Get out!"

Mills shook his head and got up. He wanted to continue to fight to get her back, but right then leaving was the best thing to do. Too much resentment lay in the center of her eyes. He had to give her time to calm down, so he reluctantly did what she asked and left without saying another word.

A few days had gone by and it was time for Farrah to return to work. Being cooped up in her room for several days had driven her insane, so returning to work was a welcome treat. Once her car was parked she grabbed her black Chanel bag from the passenger seat and got out. To her dismay, as she approached her office doors she found Mills there waiting for her.

Not today, she thought, rolling her eyes. She didn't feel like another big blow-up with him. She'd said everything she had to say the last time they came in contact. Nothing else needed to be said. It was over. The baby was gone and they were done. It didn't help that Mills's undeniable sex appeal kept calling out to her.

As she walked toward him it was almost as if time slowed. Her black Alexander McQueen heels with gold spikes clicked against the pavement as her round hips swayed from side to side.

Mills's hands were inside his tan jeans. His Nike Air Jordan Spizike sneakers shined under the light of the sun.

She hated the effect his presence had on her. The sight of him caused her to melt like hot butter. Mills was gorgeous but how fine he was didn't take away from the fact that he'd broken her heart.

"Good morning," Mills spoke.

"Hi." Farrah shielded her eyes from the sun with her hand.

"You look nice today."

"Thank you." Farrah avoided eye contact.

If she looked Mills in the eyes she'd fall right back into his arms and she couldn't afford to do that, especially after everything that had happened.

"You still mad?"

"What you think?" Farrah cocked her head to the side.

"I guess so." Mills laughed.

"I gotta get into work." Farrah went to bypass him but Mills stopped her.

"Let me talk to you."

"We already said everything." Farrah sighed.

"No, you said what you had to say. I didn't."

"What you got to say, Mills? That you're sorry for lying to me, that you didn't mean to cheat? What's gonna be the excuse today?"

"I don't have any excuses. I fucked up and ain't no changing that," he confessed. "I just want you back."

"Like I'm supposed to believe that. You didn't want me when you had me."

"It's not that I didn't want you. I didn't appreciate you. Now I realize what I had. You know I'm not really good wit' words but I love you and that's gotta be worth something."

Farrah gazed deep into Mills's eyes. The man she'd fallen head over heels in love with was back. Her gut was telling her that every word he spoke was sincere. He loved her just as much as she loved him. Maybe they could get past all of the pain and start again.

Farrah didn't want to be unhappy anymore. It was too time consuming. She wanted to feel complete and she didn't feel that way without Mills by her side. He'd become a part of her. For better or worse he was hers and she was his.

"You sure you don't have anything else to tell me? Everything is out on the table?" Farrah furrowed her brows.

"Yeah," Mills lied.

The smart thing to do would've been to tell her about the drunken tryst he had with Jade at Diablitos but if he 'fessed up he'd never have a chance with her again. They were almost a couple. He couldn't chance it by dredging up painful secrets; besides, Jade had moved on. There was no reason Farrah had to know. That night was just what it was, a night. It didn't mean anything to Mills. His love for Farrah outweighed everything, even the truth. If he couldn't have her he wouldn't be able to function. He knew what was in his heart, and the only thing that mattered was that he prove to her how much she meant to him, 'cause being without her wasn't an option.

"Okay, Mills," Farrah warned, "I'm not playin'. You better be tellin' me the truth, 'cause if we're going to do this again we need to do it right. It can't be no secrets."

"There are none," he swore.

"A'ight." She gave him a warning glance.

"You love me?"

Farrah's heart couldn't help but smile. She loved Mills more than either he or she knew.

Epilogue

Spring was in full effect and things between Mills and Farrah had fallen back into place. It'd taken a minute for her to feel all the way comfortable with him but he'd been nothing but an absolute angel. He'd been so gentle and caring. There wasn't a minute that went by when he wasn't doting on her and making her feel like the most special woman in the world.

The skate park was finally under construction and Farrah and London had four clients that they were styling for the New Now Next Awards. The sun was finally beginning to shine on Farrah again. That night as the stars shone bright in the sky she stared lovingly down at her left hand. The five-carat princess-cut diamond ring on her hand was blinding her. Over dinner that night Mills had proposed and she'd blissfully said yes.

"What you doing?" Mills crept up behind her and held her in his arms.

"Admiring my ring," Farrah gleamed.

"You know for a minute there I thought you were gonna say no."

"Why would you think that?" She turned around and hugged him.

"'Cause you were quiet for so long."

"I was blinded by all of the ice." Farrah wiggled her fingers.

"So when you wanna get married?"

"The fall will be great."

"I like the fall." Mills kissed the back of her neck. "You smell good." He cherished her scent.

"I've been thinking." Farrah bit her bottom lip nervously. "After we get married why don't we try to have another baby?"

"You for real?"

"Yeah, I'm mean I regret what I did. Like right now I would've been almost five months." She choked back the tears that filled her throat.

Mills could see the sadness in her eyes and wanted nothing more than to fix it. "Whatever you want I'm down wit' it."

"Really?" Farrah jumped up and down.

"Yes." Mills hugged her tight.

Relishing each other's touch, Mills and Farrah took in the moment. Like Bleek and Indigo from *Mo' Better Blues* they were experiencing a love supreme. Nothing could rain on their parade.

"Is that your phone ringing?" Farrah heard his phone ring in the distance.

"Yeah, let me get that." Mills reluctantly let her go and picked up his phone.

Without saying a word he stepped out onto the balcony.

"Hello?" he said in a low tone.

"Hey," Jade spoke softly.

Mills held the phone, perplexed. He hadn't spoken to her in two months. "What's up?"

"Umm . . . I'm pregnant."

Mills's entire body froze. This couldn't be happening. His worst nightmare was coming true. He'd just proposed to Farrah. She stood only a few feet away from him, blissfully unaware that at any second her world was about to crash.

Coming Soon 2014 . . .

Reckless 2:
Nobody's Girl

by

Keisha Ervin

Prologue

The sun barely kissed the afternoon sky as Farrah placed a cardboard box on top of her king size bed. For months she'd dreaded this moment. Her children had asked her repeatedly to gather her late husband's belongings since she was downsizing and moving into a small apartment. But Farrah just couldn't bring herself to do it. Her husband's things were all she had left of him.

They were her most coveted and cherished treasures. She couldn't part with them and place them into storage. It would be like acting as if he never existed, like the love they shared wasn't the kind of love stories were written about. Farrah couldn't box up a nearly fifty year marriage and tuck it away in a cold dark room. The love between her and her husband was the kind you dreamt of as a little girl. It withstood the test of time. Their love was unwavering, strong and authentic.

She'd spent half of her life with him. They'd fallin' in love quickly, fought, broke up, made up, pledged their love to God, traveled the world and bore children together. When Farrah's husband became sick with stage 4 colon cancer she was right there by his side until he looked into her eyes and took his last breathe. And even though she'd wrestled with the thought of this day for months she couldn't put off the inevitable any longer. Moving day was here. Her three children and some of her grandchildren were there helping her pack.

"Granny," Farrah's oldest grandson Ross knocked softly on the door. "You okay?"

Farrah looked up at her grandson and tried her hardest to blink back the tears that begged to fall. Ross was the spitting image of his grandfather. At twenty-three years old he was tall, charismatic and smart.

"Yeah, baby I'm okay." Farrah sat on the edge of her bed.

"I ain't know Paw-Paw had all of this stuff." Ross looked around the room in amazement.

All of his grandfathers, clothes, shoes, photos, books, awards and memorabilia from his successful career were scattered everywhere.

"Yeah, your grandfather collected a lot of things over the years." Farrah examined the room as well.

"What's this?" Ross picked up an old photo book. "I never saw this album before." He sat beside his grandmother.

Farrah looked on somberly as Ross flipped through the album.

"You and Paw-Paw look young."

"I wasn't always an old woman." Farrah admired a picture of her when she was thirty.

Although she was 81 years old gravity had been good to her. She wasn't the vibrant, youthful woman she was in the picture but for an elderly woman Farrah's beauty shown through the wrinkles and age spots on her skin. Beauty and fashion were still an important part of her life and she took pride in taking care of herself.

"Let me see that." Farrah reached out her shaky hand.

Ross handed her the photo album.

"Your grandfather was a good lookin' man." Farrah traced the outline of his face and smiled.

"Was it love at first sight when ya'll met?"

"Something like that," Farrah chuckled. "Your Paw-Paw and I had sort of a rough start."

"What happened?"

"Well," Farrah took a deep breathe and gazed out into space.

Chapter 1

You used to be sweet to me.
—Ledisi, "Turn Me Loose"

Every girl dreams of that Sex and the City moment where Mr. Big rushes to Paris to declare his undying love for Carrie, finds her, rescues her from the evil Russian, and kisses her tears away. Shortly thereafter they walk hand in hand into a life filled with Manolos, candlelit dinners, and bliss. Eight months ago Farrah James's Mr. Big, Corey Mills, aka Mills, made all of her dreams come true when he got down on one knee and put a ring on her finger. Now she was on top of the world.

Her company, Glam Squad, which she co-owned with her bestie London, was skyrocketing. Together they'd styled and done makeup for Lana Del Rey, Solange Knowles, and Rihanna. They'd even styled Lady Gaga for Vanity Fair's September issue and dressed Emma Stone for the Oscars. On top of her career successes, she and Mills were planning their star-studded multimillion-dollar wedding, house hunting, and she was considering getting pregnant again.

After a bitter breakup, Farrah aborted their first baby, but now she was more than ready to bear Mills's child. On the outside looking in, Farrah and Mills's relationship was destined to fail. For three years she'd dated Mills's best friend, Khalil, but after years of dealing with his alcoholic and mindless behavior, Farrah broke things off. Distraught over their breakup, she found solace in Mills's friendship. Over time it turned romantic, despite the fact that Mills was in a six-year relationship with his then girlfriend, Jade.

After tiring of trying to make his failing relationship work, Mills left Jade and instantly made Farrah his new woman, disregarding his doubts that they could really make it work. Soon Mills's fears came into fruition when, drunkenly one night, he slept with Jade. Mills was so torn up over his infidelity that when he assumed Farrah was cheating on him with Khalil, he kicked her out of his crib. He then went on to not speak to her for weeks, although she'd told him she was pregnant.

With nowhere to turn, Farrah did what she felt was best at the time and aborted their child. However, weeks later, after Mills learned that Jade had been cheating on him for the last year of their relationship, he begged for Farrah's forgiveness and won her back. Now eight months later, she was sitting on cloud nine. Little did Farrah know, at any moment the floor was sure to fall from beneath her feet.

It was half past one and she'd been stalling the celebrity wedding planner, Adore Phillips, for over thirty minutes. They had a ton of things to discuss, but none more important than the all-time-consuming seating chart. With the wedding only a month and a half away, she and Mills had to finalize who would sit where. Farrah tapped her black five-inch Louboutin Pigalle heels against the floor and eyed her watch again nervously.

She was supposed to be concentrating on the words coming out of Adore's mouth, but they fell on deaf ears. All she could think about was Mills. He knew how important this particular meeting with their wedding planner was. *I'm gonna kill him*, she thought to herself as Adore showed her pictures of the finalized menu cards.

"Excuse me, Adore. Do you mind if I give Mills a call? He should've been here by now."

"Sure thing, hon." Adore eased back out of her chair. "Just tell him to get his butt over here quick. I have a two o'clock appointment with Brad and Angelina."

"Okay," Farrah said, nodding.

"I'ma grab me a cappuccino. Would you like one?" Adore asked.

"No. Thank you. They give me headaches," Farrah politely declined.

"Okay." Adore closed the door behind her.

As soon as the coast was clear, Farrah picked up her phone and called Mills. To her surprise he answered on the first ring.

"What up?"

"Where are you?" she hissed.

"Stuck in traffic," Mills groaned.

"Which highway did you take?"

"I'm on Forty."

"Oh, my god." Farrah massaged her forehead. "Are you kidding me? How far away are you? Adore has another appointment at two o'clock."

"I'm going as fast as I can, Farrah," Mills sighed. "Just give me a minute."

"Okay, but hurry up." Farrah ended the call.

"Did you reach him?" Adore reentered the room with her cappuccino in hand.

"Yeah, he's on his way. He's just stuck in traffic. He'll be here any minute," Farrah assured.

Unbeknown to Farrah, Mills was not stuck in traffic. He was actually at Forest Park. Forest Park is one of St. Louis's largest and oldest parks. It was massive, so he didn't have to worry about anybody spotting him. Sitting anxiously on a park bench, he awaited his ex Jade's arrival. For the past eight months he'd been telling lie after lie. With the way things were going it didn't look like the lies were going to stop anytime soon. He couldn't fathom how not telling Farrah about his infidelity would lead to him living a double life. Since the night Jade called and dropped the bomb that she was pregnant, Mills had been secretly keeping in contact with her.

Since there was a huge possibility that Jade's baby was his, and he didn't want Farrah to find out that he'd cheated, Mills made sure that Jade's housing and medical bills were paid. He'd even gone to visit her after she'd given birth to a baby girl she'd proudly named Jaysin Cori Mills. Mills couldn't see any resemblance between him and Jaysin, but he'd continued to support Jade financially until his paternity test was done. His schedule was all booked up until after the wedding, so he'd already decided to take the paternity test after his and Farrah's honeymoom.

Mills had mixed feeling about taking the paternity test. A part of him just wanted to get the results so he could move on with his life and figure out what he needed to do next. But another part of him was afraid to find out the truth. If Jaysin was his, he had no idea if or how to tell Farrah. There was no way Farrah would stay with him and Mills couldn't have that. He'd worked too hard to win her trust back. For Mills, ending up alone seemed inevitable if he was the father. Mills was, overall, anxious about getting the paternity test done, so he could find the much-needed air to breathe or a shovel to dig his own grave.

As a slight October breeze swept over his skin, he spotted Jade in the distance. She walked with all of her weight shifted to the right because of the pumpkin seat in her right hand. Although Mills no longer looked at Jade in a loving or sexual way, he couldn't deny her beauty. Even after having a baby, sex appeal still dripped from her pores. Jade was made for the camera. She was aesthetically perfect. She stood five feet nine and her measurements were a dick- hardening 34-24-38.

Her butter-colored skin, blond buzz cut, full mouth, curvaceous hips, and ample behind made men and women turn their heads. But Mills wasn't fooled by her good looks. He knew what lay behind the surface was a self-centered, coldhearted bitch.

"Hey," she said, sitting the pumpkin seat down on the bench next to him.

"What's up?" Mills replied, drily.

"It's a little chilly out today, isn't it?" Jade rubbed her hands against her arms to create body heat.

"Yeah." Mills reached into his jacket pocket and pulled out a check. "Here." He held it out.

Jade eyed him and shook her head. Since Jaysin had been born, it was the same routine every month. They'd meet in the park, he'd hand her a check, then bounce. Mills didn't try to hold the baby or ask how she was doing or anything of the sort. It was like neither of them existed. It was bad enough that she had to go through her entire pregnancy alone. Jade figured that once the baby was born, Mills would come around, but she was sadly mistaken.

Mills didn't have anything for her but a check to keep her quiet and an attitude. Yes, she'd done him dirty and broken his heart and for the rest of her life Jade would regret her actions, but their daughter didn't have to pay for her transgressions. Jaysin deserved better. She was Jade's greatest accomplishment. From the moment she was born, Jade made a vow to be a better person.

Her needs no longer mattered. Everything she did was for Jaysin. She just wished that

Mills felt the same. Jade slipped the check from Mills's fingertips and read it. Her heart instantly dropped to the pit of her stomach. The check was only for a grand.

"Listen." She took a deep breath. "I'm not tryin' to be a bitch or get all off into your pockets, but this is not enough. I need more money."

"Excuse me?" Mills screwed up his face.

"Don't even start all of that." Jade tried to reason. "All I'm sayin' is this is not enough to cover the bills, Jaysin's doctor bills, formula, Pampers, and putting food in the house. It takes a lot to take care of her, Mills. I just need a little bit more money every month."

"You got a lot of nerve," Mills chuckled. "You need to be happy that I'm even giving you that, 'cause I don't see that other nigga giving you a dime."

Mills referred to NBA star Tyrin Rhodes, aka Rock, whom Jade had cheated on him with.

"Why would he?" Jade countered, becoming pissed. "She's not his daughter."

"That's to be determined," Mills scoffed.

"Are you kidding me? She looks just like you." Jade snatched back the blanket that was covering Jaysin's face.

Mill looked at the three-month-old baby out of the corner of his eye and saw bits of himself staring back at him. She was a gorgeous baby girl who held most of her mother's exotic looks, but her smoldering brown eyes and deep dimples reminded her of him.

"Like I said—" Mills sat up straight. "I don't know if that's my baby and neither do you."

"Oh, my god, you are unbelievable," Jade said in disbelief. "You know that she's your daughter. You just don't wanna step up and take responsibility 'cause you haven't told your so-called fiancée yet."

"What you mean, so-called fiancée?" Mills ice grilled her. "She is my fiancée and we're getting married in a month and a half, as a matter of fact."

"And that's fine Mills," Jade stressed. "I'm happy for you, but you need to acknowledge your daughter. I need your help and the money that you're giving me is not enough."

"Well, I don't know what to tell you, 'cause I'm not giving you no more money. You can forget that."

"What am I supposed to do?" Jade shrilled.

"How about get a job?" Mills shot.

"I can't. I don't have anybody to watch her." Jade felt her face become hot.

Tears were beginning to form in her eyes. There was a time when Mills would have never talked to her like this. He used to be sweet to her, but those days were long gone and Jade had no one to blame but herself.

"That's your problem. And just to let you know, when I get back from my honeymoon we gon' get all of this straight once and for all."

"Get what straight?" Jade furrowed her brows, confused.

"I'ma get a paternity test done."

"Wow," Jade said, stunned.

"I don't know what you sayin' wow for. Let's not pretend that you weren't fuckin' another nigga behind my back, let alone in my bed," Mills barked.

"Whateva, Mills," Jade said, waving him off. "Do what you gotta do, 'cause I'ma do what I gotta do."

"You do that, then." Mills stood up and placed on his shades.

As Mills walked down the trail leading to his car, Jade sat staring out into the open space. When she'd awakened that morning she hadn't suspected that things would end up this way. Mills was angry and bitter and he had every right to be. But Jade had to do what was best for her daughter, even if that meant taking things into her own hands and calling Mills's bluff.